Save Them

R. Roy
savethemsaveus.com

Cover: Designed by R. Roy in Canva

Cover photo credits: Seated couple – Artem Balashevsky, Pexels

Penguins – Freepik Premium

Back cover: Zsolti Tamasi, Pexels

Copyright ©2023 by R3 Services LLC

Second Edition

ISBN: 979-8-9929921-0-6

To Coll, without your love and support this book
may have never been written.

The ship had gone down with all hands on board. Lucas had survived the near freezing waters of the Southern Ocean. It was really George and Grace that saved him. Two of the most amazing beings he had ever met. And June. She gave him a reason to live. A reason to fight. Something to fight for.

Table of Contents

Chapter 1:

Ushuaia

Six months earlier Lucas Kalloe boarded a ship that would take him to one of the most cruel, unforgiving and desolate places on the planet. With average temperatures of 71 degrees below zero inland and a balmy 14 degrees above zero along the coast, it was mankind's latest vacation destination. A place that is 75% bigger than the entire land mass of the United States and covered almost entirely in ice.

A desert at the bottom of the world. A desert with no sand. A desert with no sun at certain times of the year. There were no palm trees, soft sand or warm ocean breezes. There was an ocean. It just wasn't an ocean you ever wanted to be in. Antarctica.

He found it curious that people would pay good money to cruise to a location such as this. Antarctica wasn't known for its wide variety of exciting excursions, unless you consider staying in a tent overnight in one of the most inhospitable places on the planet exciting. Excursions in Antarctica will get you killed, if you don't pay attention and follow the rules. It's not a vacation spot. And yet, it is.

This was his first cruise, and he was a bit apprehensive about the trip. It was late March, the end of the cruise season. The very end. Cruise ships don't travel to Antarctica from April to September. For good reason.

That's when storms are frequent and the most violent. They come out of nowhere with almost no warning. The ice covering the ocean freezes so hard and so thick, only a well-built ice breaker could make the journey. Mother Nature does her best to keep humans away during the winter months. That's when she reminds us who is still in charge.

The ship was supposed to leave port a few days ago, but a storm delayed those plans. Some of the passengers who simply couldn't wait around for days at their own expense to see if the ship would be able to make the trip cancelled their cruise and went home. With the weather forecast showing acceptable conditions for the next several days, the cruise line had been granted permission to make the trip. That's how Lucas managed to get booked on this trip. With cabins now available, the cruise line was happy to accept last-minute passengers. Lucas didn't have to pay for his cabin. His current employer took care of that.

He had been contacted four days ago for a job. The catch, if he accepted, would be that he would have to fly from Rio De Janeiro to Brazil to Ushuaia the next day. No exceptions. If the ship was able to leave port, he had to be on it.

He didn't know exactly what the job would be. That happened a lot in his line of work. He checked the weather forecast himself. It was only after confirming favorable weather conditions during their journey that Lucas agreed and took the job.

He thought about the people who had to cancel their once in a lifetime vacation. *Great*, he thought, *someone else's misfortune is now my misfortune.* Well, not exactly. Maybe that's a bit harsh. He's just not a cruise ship kind of guy. Still, he took the job, so might as well try to make the best of it. He can use this opportunity to work on his people skills. At least he can try.

The port town of Ushuaia was bustling with activity.

Located at the bottom tip of South America; it was considered the southernmost city in the world. It's not a big, industrial city. Ushuaia is quaint with no skyscrapers, no giant warehouse stores and no westernized fast food. No Taco Bell here. There was, however, a Hard Rock Café.

There were vehicles driving about, but the traffic was not heavily congested. Much of the traffic was from the locals going about their day and the businesses who needed to get from place to place to provide their services. Then there were the bright blue tour buses.

Bright blue buses ferried tourists around town so they could take in the sights at this stopover location before they departed for their next destination. People from all over the world came here to begin their vacation of a lifetime.

Ushuaia had become a tourist town, and it had a port.

Lucas had arrived in Ushuaia earlier that day after having to get on three different airplanes to get there. He walked along the streets, not really having anything else to do. He'd rather be outside taking in the scenery than sitting in his hotel room. He'd be leaving in the morning. He needed to kill some time. Besides, he'd have to eat at some point.

He saw two couples come out of the Hard Rock Cafe, chatting excitedly. He overheard them talking about their upcoming trip. *Guess I'll be seeing them tomorrow.* He continued walking and found a small restaurant on one of the back streets outside of town. The clientele inside was mostly locals. The place was not set up to attract tourists. It was very basic with tables and chairs and not much else. It was the smell that drew you in. Meat cooking on open flame. Lucas knew the scent well and he knew there was no propane or charcoal involved. The scent of the wood commingled with the meat perfectly. Asado, meaning barbeque. He didn't realize how hungry he was until he smelled that. In Ushuaia they take their cooking very seriously. Inside there were a few people that didn't look like locals. He would probably be seeing them tomorrow too.

He left the restaurant at the same time as another couple. As soon as they stepped out of the building, a kid ran by and snatched the lady's purse. He couldn't have been older than fourteen. "My passport! Our tickets!" Lucas started running after him. He chased the kid for a couple hundred feet when someone shot out from his left and made an impressive tackle. Lucas had to veer to the right to avoid tripping over them as they both went down. A mangy dog added to the commotion.

"Sick 'em!" the kid commanded. The dog started barking, but didn't attack.

Lucas charged at the dog, and it backed off, not willing to find out if he was bluffing or not. It seemed these two had pulled this stunt before. The boy had lost his grip on the purse and the contents now lay three feet away scattered on the asphalt. Lucas gathered up the purse and its contents. By now the boy and his subduer were standing, brushing themselves off.

"Let me go," the kid hissed. "You got the stupid purse back."

The stranger held one of the kid's arms. "That was a brazen stunt, kid. How many times has that actually worked?"

"What's it to you? You the police?"

"Nope."

"Then it's none of your business." The dog continued to bark, playing his role a few feet away.

"That your dog?"

"Maybe."

"Looks like you got enough problems. Beat it. I strongly suggest you come up with a new profit-making plan that doesn't involve breaking the law."

"Fine."

Lucas took some money from his pocket and gave it to the boy. It looked like he needed a good meal. Sometimes a simple act of kindness when someone needs it most can change everything. "Here. Get something to eat. Make sure the dog eats well too. He did his part."

The boy looked at Lucas, puzzled. Then looked as if he decided not to question it. He smiled, said thank you and trotted off with his dog.

"Thanks for stepping in", Lucas said to the stranger. The man was tall and thin, easily four inches taller than Lucas. If he had been chasing the boy, he would have caught him in seconds.

"No problem. A boy running with a fancy purse is usually nothing good."

"It is for him if he gets away with it."

"True. Giving him that money was a really nice thing to do. Most people wouldn't have bothered showing him a little mercy." His skin was much darker than Lucas's olive skin and he had a strong accent. Lucas thought he sounded almost Jamaican.

"We both decided to show a little mercy."

"Yeah, I guess. Maybe he'll decide to re-evaluate his life choices."

Lucas thanked him again and went back to the restaurant to return the purse to its very grateful owner.

Chapter 2:

Lucas

His chosen profession had afforded him many trips across the globe, compliments of whoever hired him. He had taken many jobs that took him far north to cold, icy waters. It was hard work. It involved a lot of isolation; and it was dangerous. It was also thrilling and insanely satisfying. More so than any other job he could think of. Deep sea diving wasn't for the faint of heart; but it showed him an alien world on the very same planet he had lived on all of his life.

Antarctica was one of the places on earth he hadn't been to. He knew that the continent was really no place for people. As beautiful as it was, humans really didn't belong there. And yet, they were.

As soon as mankind figured out how to get there, they arrived. Full of curiosity and wonder. Explorers competing to be the first to reach the South Pole. Scientists running tests on everything on the land and in the sea. All confident that they could tame the frozen tundra. No one tames Antarctica. You do your work. You run your tests. You remember every minute while you're there who has control. It's nature, not humans. At a little under 3% of the entire planet's land mass, it's Earth's last stand. The one remaining place that our planet is fighting to hold onto. For now, Antarctica still belongs to the Earth. Humans have not taken it from her yet, but they're trying.

He often struggles with accepting jobs like this. Part of him just wants humans to leave the continent alone. It's been doing fine on its own for millions of years. Humans are just going to fuck it up. They always do. In this case, the money he was offered and the lure of the unknown won out. Like the tourists on the ship, he was invading Earth's last stand for selfish reasons. He had to come to terms with that.

He contemplated this as he stood on the deck of the cruise ship he had just boarded, the Ice Dancer. He was there with tourists and staff, heading to the place that he wished no one was going to. Ever. The irony was not lost on him. So much for letting Earth keep her less than 3%.

The nature of his job mandates that he travel by boat to do his work. There's not much money in deep sea diving from shore. He's been on plenty of boats, most of them scientific vessels of varying size. That is where he is comfortable. On a vessel full of people who are doing their jobs for science and exploration. Not with a ship full of tourists expecting to get their money's worth by having mother nature keeping them entertained. He thought about the people on the ship. *News flash. Mother nature doesn't give a shit about how much money you spent for this trip. You'd better hope she's in a good mood.*

Lucas was born in a small country on the northern coast of South America. His birthplace is smaller than the U.S. state of Oklahoma. His childhood was a simple yet turbulent one. He was born after the civil war that started in 1986. Even though he didn't live through the war; he lived through the aftermath and consequences that war brings, no matter what side you're on. He lost an uncle that he only knows existed because of the few pictures that his parents showed him. His father still gets sad when he talks about the brother that he lost all those years ago.

Most of the country is still covered in the lush tropical rain forests that pre-dates man's arrival. Much of the population is still relatively poor. It's a simple life there. A place where you can go about your business without the incessant craziness that you find in the big tourist towns like Rio De Janeiro.

It's where he met his first love, the ocean.

Growing up in a country covered in rainforest allows for plenty of opportunities to explore. Lucas spent hours, days and probably months exploring with his childhood friends. He quickly discovered that he did not care for bugs and snakes. He endured so many bug bites as a child he often wondered if he would contract malaria and die. Some of his friends were absolutely enamored with the wildlife they discovered on their excursions. They would constantly bring all sorts of species to him saying, "Check this out. Look at this one!" The slimier the better. Lucas hated it.

One day while exploring, his friends found a boa constrictor that was bigger in circumference than any of their torsos. Maybe bigger than all their torsos put together. They were all still scrawny back then. It was an enormous and fantastic beast. They were a group of four, Lucas and three of his friends. His friends got the bright idea to pick the snake up. They were sure they could lift it. They were at the age when being macho was cool and the fact that they could actually die didn't occur to them. The boa quickly wrapped itself around one of his friends and started to squeeze. Within seconds the boy couldn't breathe. His friends panicked. Lucas picked up a stick and started hitting the snake, yelling at his friends to do the same. They obliged and together, after a few smacks, the snake decided he was outnumbered. He let go and slithered away into the dense foliage. Thankfully, after that ordeal, his friends weren't quite so eager to venture deep into the jungle looking for trouble.

It was the ocean where Lucas found joy. Swimming with his friends was another regular childhood activity; and the one Lucas enjoyed the most. He could spend hours in the water. Always wanting to go a little further, a little deeper. The many creatures he discovered there fascinated him. Slimy didn't bother him at all in the water.

His friends only wanted to swim and play in the water. They weren't interested in exploring it. One day while swimming Lucas spotted a bright blue fish with striking yellow trim. He was completely mesmerized and began to follow it. By this age, he had become pretty good at holding his breath underwater. He loved being in the water and would often push his lungs to their limit so he could stay under just a few seconds more.

He was thrilled that he was able to stay close enough to that fish to keep it in sight. He marveled at the multitude of beings he saw. As he spotted new creatures he had never seen before, he knew he was swimming farther out than he had ever been, but he thought nothing of it. He was having too much fun to concern himself with that. Soon the blue fish darted off and Lucas knew better than to continue to chase it. His lungs were straining. He needed to surface.

Once his head was above water, he looked around to get his bearings and immediately panicked. He was much farther out than he expected. He was so far out the people on the beach were small. Were those his friends crouched down on the beach digging in the sand? He couldn't tell. He was so focused on following that fish, he didn't realize how far he had swum or how close to exhaustion he had pushed himself. Now he knew.

The mere thought of swimming back to shore made his body ache. The kind of ache you get when you know you have to do something, but you really don't want to. You feel like the left and right hemispheres of your brain are using each other as punching bags and your body just gives up. Lucas didn't think about it like that at the time. All he knew was that he was scared and tired and suddenly the tiny piece of ocean that he was bobbing around in felt enormous.

He closed his eyes to calm himself. Not looking at the vast expanse of water between him and the beach helped. He used the darkness to erase the panic and negativity and create a blank slate. He knew what he had to do. He didn't have much choice. *You got yourself into this mess, now get yourself out.* He spun around so he was on his back, looking up at the sky. He wanted to keep his face out of the water and the sky gave him something to focus on. He started kicking and using his arms to propel himself towards the beach. His pace was slow and calm. He didn't want to wear himself out before he made it back to land.

Periodically he would spin around and look at the beach to see how much progress he'd made and to make sure that the current hadn't veered him away from his intended landing point. He had made it more than halfway back. The beach was much closer, and he could make out his friends. He was glad they were still there and hadn't abandoned him. He turned around onto his back again, looked up at the sky and continued paddling.

He continued the trek, paddling away, when something grabbed him. He immediately began to thrash like a crocodile being pulled out of the water. He didn't know what it was. His focus on the sky and rhythmic paddling had calmed him and he wasn't aware of much else. Then he heard a voice, "Easy kid, I got you. It's ok. Your friends were worried about you."

He had made it about two-thirds of the way back when his friends realized that the person they saw swimming back to shore was him. The boys started quite a stir on the beach as they were pointing, shouting "Look how far out he is. I can't believe he hasn't drowned yet." A man on the beach took it upon himself to head into the water and retrieve him. Once Lucas knew he was safe, he felt the energy leave his body. He was exhausted and couldn't wait to go home and sleep.

Chapter 3:

Surprise Passengers

Lucas stood on the deck of the ship for over an hour after they left port. There was a lot to see, and he really didn't have anything better to do. The breeze was crisp and calm. The ship passed by Hammer Island and its residents of penguins and sea lions. He saw the rusty and rotting Saint Christopher, which had served in Normandy as the HMS Justice in 1944. Thirteen years later it was grounded and abandoned where it now sat. *A ship with such a history deserves better than this*, he thought. As the Ice Dancer began its journey through the Drake Passage, Lucas decided it was time to go find his cabin.

A few minutes later he was standing outside the door of cabin 321. This was him. He took his luggage inside and spent about 20 seconds checking out his room. Then he was bored. He didn't watch a lot of TV. The only other option was to check out the ship. It was a smaller ship, which he liked. It felt more like the research vessels he was used to being on. It had a dining room and a gathering room that was basically the ship's version of a bar. There was a science room where you could learn about their final destination. He found the area where the cold weather gear was kept. Waterproof coats, boots and gloves. Those will come in handy. Lucas had brought his own cold weather gear; but it was best to have these things on board for the safety of the passengers.

After his self-guided tour Lucas contemplated going to the dining room for dinner. He didn't mind being around people, but he didn't much like talking about himself. He wasn't here for vacation, like every other passenger was. He felt very out of place.

While he was in Ushuaia, he watched couples walk together, sharing their lives and enjoying each other's company. He watched locals go about doing their jobs and taking care of business. He felt alone. He was alone. It wasn't the first time he told himself he needed to push himself out of his comfort zone and live a little more. The last time he did that his world came crashing down around him. He retreated into his safe space. There wasn't much room in his safe space for company. He kept it that way.

Lucas was in no mood to go to dinner, but he went anyway. He had to eat. He told himself that eating in his room alone was not an option. In the dining room, he sat at a round table with four other passengers. The two couples he saw leaving the Hard Rock Cafe the day before. They were chatting amongst themselves about the ship and their cabins. There was one unoccupied seat next to him. As he sat there, he heard a soft voice say, "Is this seat taken?"

His head turned toward the direction of the voice, and the first thing he saw was a soft auburn curl hanging down that brushed his nose when he turned his head. It smelled fresh and fragrant. It reminded him of being in a forest right after a rain shower.

"Oh, I'm sorry", said the voice as the curl's owner retrieved it and tucked it back behind her ear. Lucas looked up and stared into a pair of blue eyes with enough green in them to be striking against the auburn hair.

Another guest at the table smiled and said, "It's taken now. Please join us."

The soft voice with the auburn hair sat down and said "Hi, I'm June."

The other guests at the table introduced themselves. Lucas realized he suddenly felt a bit flustered, and he felt his heartbeat quicken. He also realized that everyone at the table was now looking at him, including her. He had not yet introduced himself. He hadn't said a word. "I'm Lucas", he practically blurted, anxious to no longer be the center of attention. That was enough to get the guests at the table to go back to their previous conversations. The auburn hair began chatting with a couple seated next to her. *What was her name? It has to do with summer*, he thought to himself. He played back the last few minutes in his mind. *It's a month, June, that's it. Mental note to self, don't forget her name is June.* He realized he had absolutely no idea who anybody else was at the table. He didn't know any of their names, and that was fine with him.

Dinner proceeded much like any other meal on a cruise ship. The couples began talking about how excited they were and what they were looking forward to when they reached their destination.

"I'm really hoping to see some whales," one woman commented. "I know we're at the end of the season so there may not be many but I'm still hoping".

"I just love the seals and sea lions," the other woman replied. "I'm a little nervous about the zodiac ride to shore. I'm afraid I'll fall overboard."

The two husbands were chatting with each other. Each agreeing that they were just happy that their wives had agreed to a vacation that wasn't on yet another tropical island with overpriced drinks.

"After a few vacations on a tropical island, they all start to look the same," one man said.

"Technically, we're going to a desert island," the other man replied. "I know it's actually a continent, but it's surrounded by water and classified as a desert."

Not wanting to be rude, the two ladies looked at June. "Are you hoping to see any animals when we get there?" one woman asked.

"Penguins," June replied. "In fact, I brought two with me. I've been taking care of them. I'm taking them home."

This caused everyone at the table to pause for a moment, including Lucas. Someone else was on the ship that wasn't a tourist.

"That is so exciting. How does one get a job working with penguins?" one woman asked.

"You get a degree in Ornithology. The study of birds," June replied.

"Can we see them?"

"I can't promise anything," June replied. "They're a mated pair. They were brought to the mainland together when the female fell ill. She recovered and they seemed to be doing well until recently. They both stopped eating. I managed to get permission to bring them back to the continent."

"Oh, the poor things," one woman replied. "I can't believe you're on a cruise ship with penguins," she smiled.

"It wasn't the original plan, but this is how it worked out," June said.

Then the attention turned to Lucas. He had been silent the entire time and it was his turn to contribute to the conversation.

"How about you Lucas?" a gentlemen asked.

"I'm a diver. I'm going to voluntarily jump into the freezing cold water."

One of the men motioned to Lucas and June. "I'm glad you both sat at our table. You guys are cool."

"Yeah," the other man agreed. "Now I'm thinking that taking a zodiac ride to stand on a block of ice sounds kind of pathetic." He smiled at Lucas and June. "I wish you both the best, and the penguins too."

When dinner was over and everyone started to go their separate ways, Lucas tapped June on the shoulder. "I've never been on a cruise ship. This is all very new to me and a bit unnerving. I'm nowhere close to being able to sleep. Would you like to get a drink?"

June's eyes were kind and compassionate. "I need to check on the penguins. They are my main priority." She hesitated, "You could come with me if you like."

"I would like that. Thank you. I promise to be a perfect gentleman." *So much for staying in my safe space.*

As they left the dining room, the couple from the restaurant the night before stopped them. The wife thanked Lucas again for retrieving her belongings. "I'm Anna. This is my husband Jakob." Anna was petite and thin, with long blonde hair. Jakob was tall and broad, almost burly. Her accent sounded German. She looked at June. "Did he tell you that he chased down a thief who stole my purse?

He's a keeper." Anna's smile was mischievous, and her eyes practically sparkled. Lucas felt embarrassed. June seemed impressed.

After the couple had left them, June said, "So apparently you're a hero."

"Not really. I had help. Someone else tackled the kid. Those two don't know that."

As they walked June told him about the two very special guests she had brought with her.

"The penguins are on one of the decks below. Where they keep the food that needs to be frozen or refrigerated. It's not five-star accommodations, but I think they'll be fine for the short trip."

She continued, "I spoke to the captain when I came on board. The past few days have been such a whirlwind of unexpected events, with cabins opening up at the last minute. The captain said since there are now fewer passengers than originally planned, there should be plenty of fish available for the birds. I'm hoping they'll eat it."

"No sense letting it go to waste. Do they have names?" he asked.

"Yes, George and Grace."

"Did you name them?"

"I did. When they were brought to our facility they didn't have names like you would give a pet. Animals that are being rehabilitated to be released back into the wild aren't given pet names. The whole 'don't get attached' scenario. I have been their main caregiver, and I ended up naming them. It just felt like something I needed to do. Even some of the employees who are absolutely against naming the animals softened up a bit and started calling them George and Grace."

They arrived at the level where the penguins were being kept, in the belly of the ship. It was dark and dank, compared to the upper levels which were designed to be bright and inviting. There were no windows. The fixtures were the only things providing any light. Lucas felt like he was standing in a big tin can. He didn't mind. Dark and dank is what he did for a living. He could spend the next two days right here with the penguins and be perfectly comfortable. They heard the birds squawking as soon as they arrived on the deck. Lucas didn't need to be a penguin expert to understand how stressful the situation was for them. Trapped in a cage in a strange place. *I feel your pain.* A small chuckle escaped his lips when he realized he had something in common with them.

June looked at him, questioning.

"I know how they feel," he explained.

She nodded and smiled.

They were bigger than he expected. Wearing the traditional penguin 'tuxedo', with the soft glow of orange feathers around their black heads and under their chins. At almost four feet tall, they stood nearly level with his belly button. One was a little shorter than the other. "Is this Grace?"

"Yes."

Lucas motioned to the taller one. "So this is George. They're bigger than I expected."

"They each weigh over 80 pounds. I need to feed them and calm them down for the night. I'm going to spend some time with them, just to keep them company. Please don't feel like you need to stay the entire time. I'll be fine here with them."

"I can stay. I have nothing else planned. My options are to go upstairs and sit in the bar by myself or go back to my cabin. Neither one of those sounds very intriguing right now. Thank you for inviting me to come along. George and Grace are beautiful and I'd like to help, if I can."

"Honestly, I can take care of them by myself, but I really appreciate having some human company. This dark and confining space is not my favorite place to be. I'm a little claustrophobic."

June got to work taking care of the birds. She had thrown together as much as she could during her last-minute packing job before she had to leave for the trip. She let them out of their cage so they could eat and roam around a bit. They didn't eat much. But the fish they were offered was just too good to pass up. She took some basic vitals on the birds to check their health status. Cleaning supplies had been placed nearby by crew members since pretty much all penguins do is eat, waddle and poop. Lucas got to work cleaning up. He was happy to be able to help.

Once the tasks were done they sat down and just let the birds wander. The area had been blocked off so they couldn't wander too far. There were no chairs, so they sat on the cold floor. George and Grace came over to check him out. They toddled up to him, staring as they swayed. Lucas felt like they were trying to decide if he was good enough for June. He reached his hand out slowly to pat them on the head. They allowed it.

"They seem to like you.," June said.

Two crew members stopped by to make sure everything was ok. "We're just checking on the penguins," one of them said. They left when June thanked them and said everything seemed fine.

This gave Lucas an opportunity to learn a little bit more about June.

"Was taking care of penguins your first career choice?" he asked.

"Not exactly," she answered. "I grew up in New York City. The only wildlife I was exposed to as a kid was pigeons and squirrels. I went to the zoo often, and seeing the animals there made me a little sad. I wanted to experience animals on a much bigger scale. In their natural habitat. I always loved watching the birds fly around the city. New York City is a great place, but it always felt a bit constricting to me. Cornell University has an excellent Ornithology program, so I enrolled."

"I had no idea Ornithology was the study of birds until tonight."

"Most people don't."

"How about you?" she asked. "Was diving your first career choice?"

"Pretty much. Since I was a kid. I grew up in a small country. My childhood was filled with exploring rainforests and swimming in the ocean. I was never very fond of the rainforest, but I always loved the ocean. It's where I feel calm and at peace."

"Being able to go to the ocean every day sounds wonderful," June said. "I don't consider Hudson Bay the ocean."

Lucas smiled. "I have been to many places, but I've never been to New York. Is driving there as bad as people say?"

"Yes. The streets are crowded, and parking is hard to come by. There are a lot of people walking around, which makes getting around in a car even more difficult. I had to have a car to get out of the city, so I got a Volkswagen Beetle. It's small and not highly sought after by thieves. That car got me the nickname of Junebug."

Lucas smiled. "Junebug. I like it. Would it bother you if I called you Junebug from time to time."

June paused, thinking. "It's a name that my friends and people close to me use. We're not there yet."

"I totally understand."

They just looked at each other for a few moments. Neither one knowing whether to continue the conversation or find an excuse to call it a night. He felt very comfortable with her. His breath quickened and his stomach seemed to be tap dancing. *This trip is not starting out the way I expected.*

June broke the silence. "It's time to put these two to bed. They need their beauty sleep and so do I." Lucas thought about making a comment about how she was already beautiful, but he felt that it would sound creepy, so he thought better of it. The penguins were still roaming about, investigating their new living space. Lucas calmly steered them toward the cage, where June was waiting to tuck them in.

"Penguin herding," he said with a smile.

June chuckled. George and Grace squawked a bit but seemed ready to settle down in their safe space.

As they neared the exit, June turned her head back toward the cage. "Say good night Gracie."

"Honk!" came the reply.

It was obvious that this was a regular thing between the two. Lucas could see the warmth that it brought to June's soul.

"Did you teach her that?"

"No. She came up with that on her own. It was after I had been taking care of them for a couple of days. I went to leave one night, and Grace honked as I was leaving. I felt like she was telling me she didn't want me to go. She did it again the next night. After that, I added the 'Say good night, Gracie'. It's how I came up with their names. It's been our exchange ever since."

"Would it be okay if I walked you to your cabin? Nothing more," he added quickly, not wanting her to think he was trying to get into her pants already.

A flash of uncertainty crossed her face, then she smiled and said, "I would like that." Their cabins were in the same hallway. They said good night and Lucas headed to his cabin. He knew he wouldn't be able to sleep. He took a shower and turned on the TV, paying no attention to it. Instead, playing back the events of the last few days in his mind.

Chapter 4:

Rough Seas

Lucas awoke the next morning to more than a gentle rocking of the ship. The rocking was bad enough that he realized he was rolling from side to side in bed without any effort on his part. The ship had come into bad weather. Time to find out how bad.

He got dressed, grabbed his coat and headed out to try to get some information from the ship's crew.

He arrived at a common area and found a group of passengers questioning the crew members.

Jakob Haas, Anna's husband, seemed to be leading the charge.

"We have a right to know what's going on. Is this going to get worse? Can we turn back to Ushuaia?"

"We are monitoring the weather very closely," one of the stewards responded. "Our highest responsibility is to keep our passengers safe. Please know you are our top concern. There were a few other crew members standing nearby to help calm the passengers and be ready in case the frightened crowd turned into an angry mob.

Lucas saw the purser he had spoken to the day before standing nearby. He was not currently dealing with any frantic passengers. Lucas took that short reprieve as an opportunity to pull him to the side and quietly ask him for an update.

"What are we looking at Tony? I want facts, not fluff."

"All of the reports that I have say the storm isn't expected to get so bad that we would have to consider turning back. The captain has decided to continue to the continent."

"Okay, let me know if you get any updates otherwise. Please."

"Will do Sir."

Lucas left so Tony could get back to helping calm the passengers. He needed coffee. He headed up to the dining room.

As he walked down the hallway toward the dining room, the smell of pancakes and bacon and fresh coffee filled the air.

He walked into the dining room and looked around. He had seen it on his self-guided tour the day before, but it still surprised him. The opulence was the first thing that stood out. He knew that this dining room paled in comparison to the huge cruise ships that were literally floating cities which carried more than 5000 passengers. For him, this was his first experience with "the good life". He stood for a moment, letting it soak in.

The boat was still pitching significantly. Left, then right, then up, then down. He watched the passengers struggling with their tasks. Coffee spilling. Food falling from plates onto the floor. Passengers losing their balance. It was almost comical.

Something out of the corner of his eye caught his attention. He turned to see June struggling to grab a waffle with a pair of tongs. He couldn't help but smile.

He quickly walked over. "Let me help."

"Good morning." She motioned to the container of waffles. "This has proven to be much more difficult than I anticipated."

She had everything on one of those plastic trays you get in a buffet line. The coffee had spilled, and the silverware was hanging off the plate, sliding back and forth, dangerously close to falling to the floor.

"I'll hold your tray so you can work on wrangling that waffle."

"Thanks. This is a lot of work to get breakfast. I'm not even sure I'll be able to eat it, or keep it down."

June finally got the waffle onto the plate, and they found two open chairs to sit at.

"Please join me. Are you eating?" June asked.

"I'm going to try. Coffee first. I'm going to get you more coffee too since your tray has become a coffee pond."

"Thanks."

It wasn't easy but Lucas managed to get two fairly full cups of coffee and a plate of food for himself back to the table. It took multiple trips but mission accomplished.

"Have you checked on George and Grace this morning?"

"Yes. They've had breakfast and some time out of their cage to stretch their legs."

"How are they doing?"

"Physically they seem fine, but I'm worried about them. I'm not thrilled with the current circumstances, but I do believe getting them home is the best thing for them right now. A crew member helped me secure their cage, so it won't slide around. Being locked in their cage while it slides this way and that was putting too much stress on them."

They were still sitting at the table chatting when one of the crew members came into the dining room to make an announcement.

"Ladies and gentlemen, I want to apologize for the rough seas we have encountered. I assure you that the weather forecast showed no indication of any rough weather before we left port. Storms do come on suddenly in Antarctica, and we're in one. Please stay inside and off the decks. It's not safe outside. It's a good idea to keep your cold weather gear with you when you are not in your cabin. We have games and activities available onboard."

"We didn't pay thousands of dollars to play Monopoly. My wife wants to see icebergs and whales and they're outside." It was Jakob Haas.

"It's fine," Anna said. "No one should be outside."

"Again, I sincerely apologize from the captain and the entire crew. Please let any one of us know if you need anything."

As they left the dining room Lucas heard Mrs. Hass say, "C'mon honey, let's go get our coats from our cabin."

Her husband replied, "I got a bad feeling about this."

Lucas and June ate what they could of their breakfast and left the dining room. They walked down the hallway slowly, with the ship pitching left and right and no particular place to go.

"Is there anything I can do to help you and George and Grace?"

Her eyes revealed weariness, but were still bright.

"Keep me company for a while? I can't sit in my cabin in this weather."

"Happy to. What would you like to do?"

"Well, our options are limited. Would you mind just sitting in the bar for a bit? Seems strange to go to the bar right after breakfast but I think the environment might be a good distraction. I don't feel like playing games, especially if Mr. Haas is there."

"I understand. I think it's a good idea. I'm not much of a drinker. Drinking and diving don't mix, and I never know when I'm going to get a call for a job."

"That makes sense. I'm not a big drinker either but I was looking forward to a glass or two of Chardonnay."

"Now might be the perfect time to indulge," he smiled.

They walked into the bar and looked for two empty seats.

The bar was crowded. After all, there wasn't much to do on a small ship when you can't go outside. They spotted an open table in the back corner. Two seats away from the bulk of the crowd. Perfect.

Lucas pulled out a chair for June and she sat down. "What can I get you? I'll go up to the bar and get it."

"It's too early for alcohol. I'll have a Shirley Temple if they have it."

On his way up to the bar Lucas saw Jakob and Anna Haas walk in with the coats they had retrieved from their cabin.

Back at the table Lucas offered, "Two Shirley Temples. Seemed like a good choice so I got one too."

June's seat was facing away from the bar. "I heard Jakob as soon as he walked in. Seemed like he wanted everyone to know he had arrived."

"Yeah, I saw them walk in. At least they have their coats."

Just then they heard Jakob's loud voice, "Guess there's nothing to do on this barge but drink all day."

Lucas looked at June. "This is not the calming environment you were hoping for."

"It's okay. I might not stay long but I am going to sit here and drink this Shirley Temple. It looks yummy."

They talked for the next two hours. About everything. June told him about living in New York. "There's really not that much to tell," she said. "It's a big city with millions of people living in it. It's crowded, nearly impossible to drive in and you have to stay very aware of your surroundings. There are criminals and pickpockets, just like in any big city. After I graduated high school, we moved to New Jersey. My parents were done with living in the city. They did manage to keep a small apartment near Central Park. For all of its faults, New York is still home." It was the kind of conversation you have with someone you've just met; and everything they say is a new learning experience. When your brain is taking every piece of information offered and trying to construct a complete picture of the person in your mind.

They were completely unaware of how long they had been sitting there. A waitress had brought them two more Shirley Temples while they were talking. Neither of them had moved from their chair.

Chapter 5:

Overboard

Thump. The ship shuddered.

Everyone felt it. "What was that?" Jakob asked the bartender.

"Most likely an iceberg. We probably grazed one."

"Those things?" Jakob said, motioning to the window. "They're not that big – and we're not close enough to hit one."

"They are much bigger under water than what you see on the surface."

Lucas looked out the window. The storm was pushing ice into their path. On the surface, it didn't seem like much; but Lucas knew the bartender was right. There was a lot more ice under the water that they couldn't see.

Thump! The ship shook harder. That one was on the port side, the side they were on. Thump! That one came from the starboard side. The ice was closing in on both sides of the ship.

Shit.

Jakob looked at his wife, who was visibly distraught. "C'mon honey, let's go for a walk." Anna seemed fine, but Jakob staggered out of the bar. He'd had too much to drink.

Tony walked in as the Haas's were walking out. He was checking on passengers and crew throughout the ship. He gave the couple a concerned look.

Lucas got up and told June he'd be right back. He wanted to see if Tony had any updates. Before he could talk to Tony, a lady walked up to them. "On my way here, I saw some guy going outside. Pretty sure he's drunk. Just thought I would let you know. Feel free to leave him there. It's his funeral."

"Was he tall with sandy blonde hair? Probably in his forties?"

"Yep, sounds right."

"Mr. Haas.", Tony said.

"I'll go with you."

By now June had joined them. "I'm coming too."

"Ma'am, it's not safe. I can't allow passengers out onto the deck."

June motioned her head to Lucas, annoyed. "Are you going to let him go out on deck?"

Tony said nothing. He just turned and walked out of the bar.

As they left the bar, Lucas offered his hand and motioned his head toward the water. "We're going to keep hitting those." June took his hand and held on tight.

As they headed out on deck, Tony spoke into his two-way radio. "I got a report of a passenger on deck. I'm going to check it out. Mr. Kalloe and Ms. Hewitt are with me."

"You gotta be kidding me.", came the voice at the other end. "Do you know who it is?"

"I got a pretty good idea."

"Do I even need to ask?"

"Nope."

Getting out onto the deck was a task on its own. They had to keep their balance while swaying back and forth. They stayed inside and used the windows until they spotted Jakob. He was leaning over the railing. Lucas wondered if he was throwing up. He hoped he was throwing up.

As soon as they stepped out onto the deck, Lucas saw Anna to his left. She had herself braced up against a pole for support. She was terrified.

She saw them. "I can't get him to come back inside." It was cold and windy. Spray from the waves made the deck wet and slick.

Lucas was furious. He wasn't mad at Anna. He was mad at Jakob for putting all of them in this position. The fact that neither one of them had gone overboard was a miracle. Anna was ten feet away. There would be nothing for him to hold onto to get to her; and there would be nothing to hold onto until they got back to the door.

Shit.

"Tony, I don't think both of us should be out there at the same time. Stay here. I'm going after Anna. June, please stay inside."

June nodded. She didn't like it, but she knew there was nothing she could do out on deck.

"What if Jakob goes overboard?" Tony asked.

"Like the lady said, 'It's his funeral'. Maybe Anna will be better off."

Tony shot him a look that said, *That was harsh, but you're not wrong.*

"Anna, I'm coming to get you."

"What about Jakob?"

"One at a time. You first."

Lucas started making his way toward her. Looking for anything that he might be able to grab onto if he lost his balance. As he started moving toward Anna, he saw Tony moving in the opposite direction. He knew there were emergency supplies nearby. Tony was preparing for the worst. Smart. June stayed inside, watching through the window.

Jakob was still looking at the ice, his hands locked onto the railing. His back to them. "Anna, you need to come see this. It's so cool. I brought you here so you could see icebergs. This one's really close. You gotta come see."

Anna stayed quiet. When she didn't respond, Jakob turned to make sure she was still there, where she should be. His wife by his side. Well, not quite by his side, but close enough.

Jakob saw Lucas moving toward her. He had been so focused on the view that he hadn't noticed Lucas come onto the deck.

"Stay away from my wife!" Jakob was very drunk. And very angry.

"Jakob, she's not safe here," Lucas yelled into the wind. "I'm just going to help her over to the door where it's safer. You want her to be safe, don't you?"

"I can keep my wife safe. We don't need you. Stay away from her!" Jakob started walking toward them. He could barely stand up, let alone keep his balance while the ship rocked back and forth. And yet, he was.

Lucas hoped he would fall. If he fell, he would just slide down the deck into the railing. He might get some bruises, but that's about it. If he made it up the deck to him and Anna, it would be much worse.

Physically, Lucas couldn't handle both Jakob and Anna. Not here. Tony wasn't nearby to run interference. He had to make a choice. He could move back to the door, away from Anna. That might calm Jakob down.

Jakob glared at Anna and started moving toward her.

Lucas made his decision. He had to try to get to Anna first, which he did. Jakob stumbled but managed to keep his feet on the deck by bracing himself with his hands on the deck floor. He stood up and kept coming.

Why doesn't this guy just fall already?

As expected, when Jakob reached them he started swinging. Lucas blocked the sloppy punches easily. Then Jakob grabbed Anna's fur coat and pulled. Anna screamed and tried to wrap her arms around the pole, but Jakob was too strong.

The only thing Lucas could do was grab Anna and hold on tight. He tried to use the pole as a weight, something to hold them in place. Jakob's rage seemed to give him super strength. Now all three of them were on the deck with nothing to hold onto, except each other.

Tony, I need you!

"Hey, let them go." It was the stranger who had tackled the boy the night before.

"Beat it, beanpole," Jakob spat. "This doesn't concern you. This is between me and my wife. Take your loser friend with you."

The man was agitated. He didn't like bullies, and he didn't like Jakob. He couldn't just stand there. The three of them could be swept overboard at any moment. He inched toward them slowly.

"I mean it, asshole. Back off!"

Lucas talked calmly. "Jakob, let's get Anna to safety. Come with us. You need to take care of your wife, and she needs to be inside."

"I can't go in there!" Jakob screamed. "I can't sit inside waiting to die. I can't be trapped in a room waiting for it to flood, so my last breath fills my lungs with water. I can't watch Anna die. If this ship goes down, I'll be right here. Maybe Anna and I can get onto that iceberg. Maybe help will come. Maybe we'll be saved."

Now Lucas understood. Jakob was handling his fear in a very bad way. It all made sense.

"Jakob," Lucas continued, "we're not in any danger of sinking. You knew bad weather was a possibility before you even got on board. The captain knows what to do. We're going to be fine. Anna hasn't seen any penguins yet. I happen to be friends with two penguins that would love to meet her. We can go inside, and I can introduce you."

Anna still said nothing. She had been looking at the deck floor the entire time.

Jakob calmed down. He could be the hero who introduced his wife to some penguins. He still had his phone. He could take pictures and show his friends when they got home. Now that Lucas had convinced him that they might make it home. Anna with penguins, wearing her fur coat. That might be the only good thing he gets from this trip.

Jakob spoke softly, as if speaking to a child. "Honey, would you like to meet the penguins?"

"Yes."

They had been standing on the deck with nothing but their body weight to keep them upright. Lucas's legs ached. He knew Anna was exhausted. He figured Jakob's legs probably felt like the consistency of Jell-O by now.

"Everybody ok? Need some help?" It was Tony, carrying ropes and rescue gear.

Jakob's eyes flashed with rage.

Shit.

"No, we don't need any help. I'm taking my wife to meet the penguins." He yanked Anna's arm to move her toward the door.

As soon as Anna's weight shifted, she could no longer hold her feet on the deck. Her legs gave way, and she fell into Jakob. Jakob couldn't withstand the extra weight pushing him over. The ship rocked. The water got closer, and the railing got shorter. They were in a free fall towards the railing, and the freezing water beyond that.

It all happened so fast.

There was nothing to do now but hold onto Anna. Lucas didn't want to lose her when they hit the water. Grabbing the railing was not an option. They sailed right over it.

For an instant Lucas thought about the ice that was under the water. If we slam into that, it's lights out – permanently.

Jakob lost his grip on Anna.

Lucas saw him hit the water first. That's when he realized the stranger was there. He had reached for them, got a handful of Jakob's coat, and came along for the ride. Lucas didn't see him hit the water.

"Hold your breath!" he yelled to Anna. They hit the ice-cold water; he held onto her as tight as he could. Hitting the water felt like being electrocuted. Lucas had never been electrocuted, but he imagined it probably felt something like this. He felt himself going into panicked survival mode as his body went into shock.

Fight it. Push through this. Save Anna.

As soon as they hit the water, Anna got a lot heavier. Her fur coat, now saturated, was dragging them down, fast. Lucas wrapped his arm around her waist and used his free arm to wrestle her out of the coat. It was a wrestling match. Anna was thrashing out of sheer panic and shock. She punched him. Twice. The fact that Lucas was trying to save her didn't even register in her mind. He got the coat off. Anna went still.

Shit.

He broke the surface, holding Anna's limp body. She was deathly pale, and her lips were blue. She wasn't breathing. He was facing away from the ship.

He spun around, scanning the water. The waves made it hard to see and hard to breathe. He kept getting a face full of cold salt water. Where was Jakob and the other guy? Where was Tony? He saw rescue gear hanging down the side of the ship.

Thank you Tony! He also saw Tony and several crew members standing at the railing.

Saving Anna came first, but he still wanted to know where the other two were. He scanned the water as he swam toward the ship. He was almost there when he saw the stranger's head break the surface, dragging an unconscious Jakob. He got Anna strapped into the rescue gear and yelled to Tony. "She's not breathing!"

"Got the doc here. We'll get to work on her."

Lucas swam to the stranger, who had already made it most of the way. They got Jakob strapped into the gear once it came back down.

"Fortunately, he is breathing.", the stranger yelled up. He looked at Lucas. "Here I am trying to save the guy and he's fighting me the entire time. I had to knock him out. He's nearly twice my size. It wasn't easy. It took a few punches. He nearly killed us both."

"Glad you're okay."

Lucas knew his body temperature was dangerously low. He was shaking uncontrollably. A body's survival tactic. The other guy was shaking too. The gear came back down.

"Go," Lucas said, between his chattering teeth. "I've got more muscle mass than you. I can hold out another minute or two. Just hurry up. I'm freezing."

The stranger wasn't about to waste time arguing. That would only keep them in the water longer. He scrambled into the gear so they could send it back down for Lucas. Lucas held onto the life preserver in the water, waiting for his turn.

When the gear came back down for the last time, Lucas didn't have enough dexterity in his fingers to get into it properly and secure it. He just threw himself onto the strap, so it rested under his armpits. Then he yelled "Pull", and hung on as tight as he could.

They hoisted him up. Once he was high enough, two crew members reached out to grab him and pull him in. He hadn't cleared the railing when he let go. His top half spilled over the railing, and he crumpled onto the deck. The crew members held on and made it a softer landing. He could barely move. He could barely think.

He looked over and saw Anna, wrapped in a thin silver blanket. It looked like something out of a sci-fi movie. She had a resuscitation mask on her face.

The doctor was squeezing the balloon on the mask, trying to get air into her lungs. Two crew members ran up with a gurney.

"Let's get her to the med center." the doctor said.

Tony squatted next to them. "Can you guys walk? You need to go to the med center too." He was holding two silver blankets.

"Yeah."

Jakob had regained consciousness. His previous rage was gone. He just stared at the floor. Two crew members tried to help him up. He shrugged them off. He got up and started walking, still staring at the floor. The crew members stayed close behind, saying nothing.

On the way to the med center Tony said, "You two must have been cats in a previous life and you didn't use all nine of them. It's amazing that you're still alive."

"We do make a pretty good team," the stranger said.

The walk to the med center felt like it took forever. It was on a lower level. Neither one of them had the strength to fight the rocking of the ship, but they did it anyway.

They heard the doctor and staff working on Anna in the med center. "Get an IV going. Do we have a pulse?" Then they heard "Clear!", followed by the sound of paddles electrifying Anna's chest. "Nothing? Try again. Take it up to 300."

Lucas felt nauseous. He walked into the med center and Tony came out. "They don't need me in there. I'm just taking up space. I'm going to get a weather update."

Inside, Jakob was sitting on the floor. It was easier to sit on the floor than in a chair at this point. Jakob had some sort of electrolyte drink. Lucas saw two more nearby. He assumed they were for them.

Jakob spoke, "I'm going to sue this cruise line for every penny it has."

"For what?"

"For killing my wife!"

Lucas had all he could take of Jakob's pompous attitude. "Don't even try it. That was all you. You are the sole reason we ended up in the water. You are the reason Anna is lying on that gurney. I will testify to that in court."

"Me too," the stranger added.

I really should know this guy's name, Lucas thought.

Jakob looked defeated. His last micron of pride stripped away. He began to sob. "I wish you hadn't gotten her purse back. Then we would have never gotten on this fucking boat."

Lucas stayed silent. Jakob still didn't know that the stranger had been the one to tackle the boy. Now was not the time to bring it up.

Two more thumps of the paddles. Each one making Lucas's skin crawl more than the last. He knew Jakob couldn't listen to much more of this.

Another thump.

Please, let this work. How much more can she take?

"I've got a pulse!"

Lucas breathed a sigh of relief.

Jakob put his face in his hands and sobbed. "Thank you," he said over and over, rocking back and forth.

Crew members came to check on him. Lucas motioned them away. "Let him get through this his way. He needs to process."

Once Lucas and the stranger were checked over and cleared, they left the med center. "I'm Sulieman by the way."

Lucas extended his hand. "Lucas. Thanks for helping me out. Twice. I don't think I could have saved them both without you."

"The thought to not save him did cross my mind."

Lucas didn't respond. He knew the thought would've crossed his mind too.

Chapter 6:

Truck Ride

Twelve-year old Tosin Manko was hiding in the back of a truck, trying to survive. He had run away from his village. He didn't care if he died in the back of that truck. As long as he didn't die in the village he was born in.

Being born in Niger to a poor family felt like a curse. Tosin believed his family was cursed and maybe the whole damn country too. His sister, Sanda, had been raped at fourteen years old. She was fifteen when she died giving birth. Her screams were unbearable. Tosin walked as far from the village as he dared to get away from his sister's constant screams. It was dark. He sat down in the dirt and dust and rocked back and forth. He tried not to listen. At least they weren't as loud here. He tried to occupy his mind with something else. Anything else. Eventually the screaming stopped, only to be quickly replaced by the wails of a newborn child. The baby survived, but without proper food or medical treatment, she did not live long. There was no woman in the village who could breastfeed the child. There was no store to go to for formula. The baby screamed until she passed out from pure exhaustion. She never woke up. There was no way to save her. Tosin slept outside in the dirt that night.

The relief mission showed up the next day. It wasn't the first time a relief team had visited their village. They came a few times a year with food, supplies, medicine, doctors and teachers. If they had arrived one day earlier, Sanda and the baby might still be alive. Maybe it was for the best. It saved Sanda from a life of poverty, raising a child she didn't want. Having a child without a husband made Sanda an outcast, even though it wasn't her fault. If no man claimed her for a wife, she would have been seen as fair game to the men in the village to do with her as they wished. Their father was dead. She had no man to protect her or fight for her honor.

Members of the relief team helped bury the bodies. They listened as different people recounted the events that resulted in the deaths of two members of the village. Each adding their own personal opinions and circumstances, whether real or imagined. Tosin's mother stayed quiet, letting the other villagers fill in the details. She still had mouths to feed, minus one.

Tosin's mother, Zara, had been quiet since their father left the village to fight in the Tuareg Rebellion and never came home. He left her with four children to feed and very few options. He said he was going to fight for a better life for them all. Tosin was eight at the time. He didn't fully understand the severity of his father's actions. Leaving to fight for a better life for them sounded like a noble cause. At first he thought of his father as a hero. Over the years he watched his mother's health deteriorate. She wasn't much more than skin and bones. Making sure her children ate even when she couldn't was slowly killing her. As he got older, he started to see his father's actions as a form of abandonment. His father knew he was leaving Zara without a husband. He knew what that meant. He left anyway. Even though those actions cost his father his life, Tosin still thought he did it for selfish reasons. Since Zara's husband died fighting for the betterment of the people, the men in the village left her alone. Her husband's sacrifice had earned her respect. She was not to be touched unless it was her choice. Tosin thought that was the only good thing that came from his father's desertion.

Eventually his mother did choose a new husband. Tosin was sure she did it so her children could survive. Zara simply couldn't do it on her own. She needed a provider and a protector. It would come with a price.

His stepfather, Yaro, was gruff and uncaring. He was also a widower who had lost his wife. His children were grown. That made it easier to provide for Zara and her children. It was obvious he did not care for her children. Tosin didn't think he cared about his mother either. He took her as his wife for the purpose of having a mate. It was more like a business transaction than a marriage. Tosin didn't know who the father of his dead niece was, but if he found out it was Yaro, he wouldn't be surprised.

All of this and so much more was why he had to leave. He couldn't die here. He just couldn't.

After burying the bodies, the mission team went about their business. They distributed food and fresh water. They set up tents. Doctors provided medical care. Teachers schooled the children. Most of the villagers spoke Hausa, and some French. The teachers would teach French and English to the children. They brought books and computers. No one in the village owned a computer and the mission team never left any behind when they packed up and departed. For a short time, however, the children and the rest of the village got to see images beyond their imagination. They learned about things they didn't even know existed. It was magical.

When Tosin was younger his mother insisted he attend classes when the relief team was in the village. He didn't understand why. "Why do I need to learn English?" he would ask in Hausa. Zara never gave him an answer that he found acceptable. The first time he sat at a computer and watched the world come alive right in front of his eyes, he had his answer. He heard a voice in his mind say, *Because you're not supposed to stay here.* He didn't know where the voice came from. Did it come from him? Was it a wish? A foolish dream? A stupid thought that would never come true? Tosin chose to believe that the voice was real and that it was preparing him for the path he would one day take. It gave him something to hold onto. The hope that maybe he wouldn't die in this village. That maybe he would get a chance at a better life.

He thought about that day as he sat in the back of the truck. He had never been anywhere. Never left his village. He closed his eyes and spoke to the voice in Hausa, "Please help me. I don't know what to do." He was cold, hungry and terrified. He had to trust the voice. He had to trust himself. There was no going back.

Tosin's plan to run away started to formulate at Sanra's burial. He didn't recognize it as a plan at the time. He hated his life. He hated being a burden to his mother. He hated being one of the reasons Yaro complained about having so many mouths to feed. He hated watching the mission team come in with their wonderful gifts, knowing that when they left, those gifts would go with them. He wanted to know what was beyond his village. He knew there was magic. At least some form of it. He had seen it on the computer screen. He needed to find it. He needed to know more. He needed to *live*.

He started paying closer attention to the mission team. What they did. What supplies they had and where they stored them. He paid closer attention to their conversations. Going so far as to hide somewhere close so he could listen. He struggled to understand them since they spoke English, but he understood enough to learn what day they were leaving and where they were going.

As the team packed up, Tosin used the commotion to set up his escape. He picked which vehicle he would hide in. He offered to help. This gave him an excuse to be around the vehicles. While the team made trips back and forth, loading the vehicles, Tosin hopped in the back of the vehicle he had chosen and moved a crate that had already been loaded. It was not the best use of the available space. That was the intent. Tosin hoped the loaders either wouldn't notice or would be too busy to get in the back to move it. If things went according to plan, that would give him some available space to hide in.

He kept close watch on the truck while he happily helped carry items and thanked the team for everything that they had done for his village. He used the opportunity to practice English. He knew he was going to have to speak English from now on; and the team kindly corrected him when he made a mistake. When he saw his chance, he hopped in the back of the truck and scurried towards the back. He was severely underweight so getting back there was easy. Thankfully, no one had moved the crate. He had a hiding space that couldn't be seen by anyone standing outside looking in. A short time later, the rolling door came down and latched. It was dark. He was scared. For a moment, he panicked. He almost started banging on the walls of the truck to get out. He was leaving everything he had ever known. He had no idea what would happen to his mother or siblings. He had no idea what would happen to him. He calmed himself. *Trust the voice. Trust yourself.*

He was locked in the back of the truck for three days. No one opened it during the entire trip. A few times a day the truck would stop, and the occupants would get out. He would hear them talking. He did his best to try to understand what they were saying. It gave him something to focus on. The last stop of the day was the longest when the team would sleep. Tosin didn't know if they were sleeping in the truck or somewhere else. He just knew it would be several hours before they were moving again.

Tosin had picked the truck because it carried food and blankets, along with other treasures. Back in his village, he had heard members of the team saying that they needed to bring some food and supplies with them to Tripoli. He had no idea where Tripoli was, but apparently it was very far because they weren't there yet. The truck had vents on the walls near the top. He was very grateful for the little bit of fresh air and sunlight that they provided.

He found the food that had been loaded onto the truck. He found water too. There was more than enough for one boy. Tosin had never seen so much food at one time in his entire life. It wasn't fresh food, like he was used to eating. It was in packages. These packages had been handed out in his village. He knew which ones he liked. For the first time in his life, he ate until he couldn't eat anymore. It wasn't until he was painfully sick that he realized there is such a thing as eating too much. He didn't think that was possible until that moment.

He studied the equipment that he was travelling with. He played back the last few days in his mind. He was amazed to find that if he really focused, he could remember what the team did to operate the equipment. He could remember each step, in sequence. He didn't know what it meant, but he knew how to do it.

He found a laptop and squealed with delight when he pressed the power button, and it turned on. No one heard him. He remembered what the teacher did in class. Soon the screen lit up with bright colors. He remembered to check the little picture that the teacher said was the battery indicator. It looked full. He was grateful he had this little piece of magic to keep him company.

At the end of the third day, the truck stopped as usual. Tosin expected that this was the time for the occupants to sleep and that the whole process would start again in the morning; but this time was different. There were new voices.

Tosin strained to listen, trying to understand what was going on. He heard several new voices and doors opening and closing. Had they made it to Tripoli? He heard voices move to the back of the truck. The latching mechanism started to move. Suddenly the door rolled open. It was late in the day, close to dusk.

Tosin froze. He would be found sooner or later, he knew that. At least he had made it out of Niger.

One of the men who had been at his village hopped into the back of the truck. He was called Esraa. He was talking to someone about what supplies were on the truck. Naming items off one by one. He said they had a list. As he moved around the back of the truck, pointing to each item, he noticed the empty space nestled among them. Puzzled, he leaned over a little farther and looked down – right into the tear-filled eyes of a scared twelve-year-old boy.

Esraa's immediate reaction was anger. This is not at all what he expected to find.

"What are you doing in here? You don't belong here!" Seeing the empty food packages strewn about and the laptop out of its container, he shouted, "What have you done?" Then he added, "It smells terrible in here. You've been in here for three days?"

Tosin whimpered, "I'm sorry. I had to. I couldn't watch my mother die. I couldn't die there. Not there."

Esraa's face softened. He knew this boy. Esraa was one of the men who lowered the bodies into the grave at his village. He knew exactly what this boy had been through. He also knew the boy wasn't wrong. He mumbled softly, almost to himself, "We take our teachers and our technology to these places and then we leave. What do we expect? We show them amazing things and then just expect them to forget and go back to starving to death? This was bound to happen sooner or later."

Tosin heard and he understood. He knew Esraa understood too. He also knew he was still in trouble, but maybe they'd go easy on him.

Tosin knew it was time to face the consequences of his actions. He was scared, but he couldn't wait to get out of the back of the truck. As he stood, he swayed and stumbled. He was confused. Why aren't his legs working?

Essra understood. After three days of very limited movement in the back of a fully packed cargo truck, Tosin's muscles were stiff. Esraa held his arms out. "Let me help you. Grab onto me." Esraa lifted him over the equipment. "You weigh practically nothing. I'm amazed you survived the trip. You're a fighter.
"

Esraa hopped out of the truck with Tosin in his arms. "Found a stowaway."

"What the heck? Tosin, what are you doing here?" It was the teacher from the team, Irena.

David, the doctor from the team stepped forward. "He's been in there for three days? Let's get him inside so I can take a look at him. He made it this far. I'm not going to let him die right here."

"Are we in Tripoli?" Tosin asked using the best English he could.

Esraa spoke, "You knew where we were going? You had this planned. You're smart, kid. Yeah, we're in Tripoli."

"I found Tripoli on the computer. I practiced English too," Tosin said proudly.

The team guided Tosin toward a building. Tosin looked around, trying to take everything in. It was too much to take in all at once. He had never seen anything like it, except for on the computer. There were buildings and cars and people and lights and noise. So many noises. A nearby car slammed on its brakes, tires squealing. Tosin ducked and grabbed Irena's arm, terrified.

"It's okay. That's just a car. Cars make that noise when they stop too fast," she said.

The squealing tires brought back a memory that Tosin did not want to remember. Once again, he could hear his sister's screams as she died. Tears started streaming down his face.

"Hey, you okay?" Irena asked.

Tosin nodded, shaking.

"You've been through a lot. Let's go inside." Irena took his hand.

The building they were walking toward was the most beautiful thing Tosin had ever seen.

It was all white with a tall extension on the roof. It had lots of doors and windows. There were five archways at the front that you walked through. There was a bigger building behind it that wasn't nearly as beautiful. In fact, none of the other buildings that Tosin could see were as beautiful. This one looked special. Tosin stopped and stared. The team leader, Eman, crouched down next to Tosin. "This is a mosque. It's where people pray. My friends are here. They'll help us."

Tosin nodded and they walked inside.

They walked into a huge room. It had several pillars throughout. Pillars bigger than a person. Bigger than 2 people! There were people sitting on the floor. The floor wasn't dirt. It had a soft covering over it that looked very comfortable. Much better than dirt. The people weren't talking. Tosin assumed they were praying. *All of this, just so people can pray?*, he thought to himself.

A man approached them. Eman walked forward to meet him. The two men began talking in hushed voices. Tosin couldn't understand them. Eman gestured toward Tosin. Neither of them seemed to be angry. Tosin hoped the stranger wouldn't throw him out onto the street. Eman said the people here would help. Maybe he was lying. Tosin wondered if they were trying to decide his punishment for what he had done.

The stranger approached, "Hello Tosin. I am Samir. I am one of the Imams here. You are in a safe place. We are going to help you."

Eman turned to David. "Do you want to look him over before we get him cleaned up and fed?"

"Yes," David replied. "Just a few quick basic tests. I can be more thorough later."

After the doctor was done, Eman took Tosin's hand. "Now the fun begins," he said with a smile.

Irena approached them. "Tosin, you're going to stay here. You'll be safe here. They'll take care of you. The rest of us are going to leave. Just for tonight. We have work to do. I will see you tomorrow. Ok?"

Tosin didn't want them to go. He wanted to be surrounded by people he could trust. He felt so alone. "Ok," he said.

The group turned to leave and Eman led Tosin further into the mosque. They walked into a room with bright silver fixtures. This room didn't have soft covering on the floor. The floor was hard and cold. Eman set down the items that he had been carrying. Samir had brought them. It looked like clothing.

"We're going to get you cleaned up. I'm going to help you get washed," Eman said.

Eman moved to one of the silver fixtures and turned a lever. Water came pouring out. It startled Tosin. He had never seen water like that before. He backed up so fast that he fell on his butt. It hurt.

Eman helped him up. "It's going to take some time to get you acclimated to your new life. There is much you need to learn."

Chapter 7:

Hostage

June was waiting for Lucas when he came out of the med center. "June, this is Sulieman."

June looked at Sulieman. "Can I give you a hug?"

Sulieman looked surprised and a little uncomfortable. "Sure."

June gave him a big hug. He was several inches taller than her. "Thank you so much. You could've let go of Jakob's coat. I am so glad that you are both okay." She hesitated, "Anna?"

"They got her back. I think she'll make it."

June breathed a sigh of relief.

"Have you checked on George and Grace?"

"Not since this morning. I was going to figure out how to bring them up from below, but now that the storm is letting up, I think they'll be okay. I need to go check on them."

"I'll go with you. I just want to find Tony first."

They walked around the ship until they found Tony. His face was ashen. Whatever it was, Lucas knew it wasn't good. "Is it Anna?" Lucas asked.

"No, she's going to make it, as far as I know." Tony looked like he was about to throw up. He looked at them both, obviously wrestling with a decision. He took several steps, out of earshot of anyone nearby. Lucas and June followed. Tony took a deep breath. *What now?*

"There's a killer on board. One of the cabin stewards was just found, strangled to death."

Shit.

June gasped.

Lucas felt sick. "Tell us what you know."

"She was found in a storage closet near the rooms that she cleans. She was in the back corner, covered up. It looks like a rush job. I don't think killing her was the original plan. I'm thinking she was in the wrong place at the wrong time."

"Most likely walked into somebody's cabin and saw something she wasn't supposed to see. Who knows about this?"

"You two, the doctor and the captain; as far as I know. We're keeping it quiet for now. Lucas, the crew isn't trained for this. It's a cruise ship, not a fucking battleship. We have no idea what we're up against. We don't know who. We don't know why. We don't know anything. Is it only one killer? More than one? All we know is someone is dead, and it wasn't an accident." Tony was doing his best to hold himself together.

Lucas wanted to scream. He wanted to punch his fist through the wall, grab the killer and wring his neck. Or she. It would be psychologically harder for him if it was a she. *Keep it together. Focus.*

"The killer is most likely protecting something," he said. "Some kind of secret. Can you think of anything out of the ordinary about this trip? Did any strange cargo come on board? Did you notice any unusual behavior from any of the passengers? Did any of them seem 'off'?"

"Lucas, this whole trip has been out of the ordinary. The first person I think of when it comes to unusual behavior is you."

Tony had a point. He had felt uncomfortable and out of place when he boarded. That is unusual behavior for someone going on a cruise.

"What about luggage and cargo? Did you see anything that could be suspicious?"

"Not that I can think of. We don't expect people to bring missile launchers on board hidden in telescope cases."

Lucas was still thinking. "It's also possible something was brought on board while the ship was being loaded. It could be an inside job. Do you know every crew member well? Are there any new ones on this trip?"

"Yeah, there were three new guys at the loading dock that I had never met before we left port. What kind of contraband does someone bring to Antarctica? What are they gonna do? Get the penguins hooked on crack?"

Tony had a point. Lucas couldn't think of any reasonable explanation to smuggle something into Antarctica. There's nothing there but research bases. And at this time of the year, there were very few people. Maybe that's part of the plan. No one around to get in the way, like the cabin steward. "We need more information."

"Agreed. The passengers can't know about this. I don't know how to protect them. Should I order everybody into the dining room or keep them spread out? Maybe putting everybody all in one place makes them sitting ducks."

"Moving them would probably raise suspicion. Best to act like nothing has changed. I know this sounds heartless, but it's best to leave the body where it was found, if possible. Once the killer knows we found it, he'll know we're onto him, or her, or them."

Tony closed his eyes, accepting the truth. "Agreed. It will buy us some time."

"Have you talked to the captain?"

"Yeah. We've been in contact with some ships that were leaving the continent. I'm told they're standing by in case we need help."

"What do you want to do?" Lucas asked.

"I want to start in the area that Lucia was responsible for. Lucia was the cabin steward."

"Okay, let's go."

"We're going to hang out around the ship for a while, like nothing has changed. I don't want to go straight to Lucia's area and start snooping."

"That's going to be hard, doing nothing. You want me to just follow you around for a while?"

"No. That will look suspicious. Meet me in the science center at 5:00. Hopefully most of the passengers will be in the dining room or the bar or anywhere but their cabins."

"June and I are going to get the birds. Sorry Tony, but ship rules no longer apply. They can't stay down there. It's not safe. I won't have June going below to take care of them."

Tony raised his arms halfway up in defeat. "Fine. You're right. They can't stay there. There's a service elevator we can use to bring them up. The dining crew uses it to bring the food up. We'll need an excuse."

"We can dump some of the cleaning supplies," June said. "Say we can't leave them down there in a chemical spill. If anybody goes down there, the reason will be legit."

"That should work."

They stopped by the dining area so Tony could tell the staff that the penguins needed to be brought up. The crew seemed a bit perplexed, but pleased that they would soon be able to see two of the cutest passengers on board. They were happy to stand by and help bring the birds up safely.

Lucas and June headed below deck to George and Grace. June grabbed the supplies she had brought to take care of her patients. She found two empty boxes. She threw frozen fish into one and fruit into another. They got the cage into the elevator while George and Grace voiced their discontent at being further tossed around just when things were starting to calm down. They made their way back to the dining area to find George and Grace talking excitedly to their new admirers. They borrowed a dolly and wheeled the birds to June's cabin. They got many surprised and inquiring looks as they rolled the cage down the hall.

"There's been a spill down below," June explained. "Smells terrible. I couldn't leave them there. It would make them sick, maybe kill them."

"We got the purser's permission," Lucas added. What they said was true. They just omitted the fact that they were the ones to cause the spill.

"I'll stay here with them for a while. Let them calm down." Then she whispered, "Do you think texting is safe?"

"I don't know. Just keep the texts normal."

"I'm going to try to acquire a few more ice buckets for the fish. I'll be careful."

"I don't want to leave you, but I have to figure this out. Text me so I know you're okay."

June's face softened. She gave him a warm smile. "Lucas, you can call me Junebug. From time to time."

"Ok, Junebug." He left her cabin feeling like the heels of his feet had just sprouted wings.

Lucas showed up at the science center at 5:00, carrying a bottle of beer. Tony was already there and looked at the bottle with an inquisitive expression.

"I'm trying to look like a passenger, not a bodyguard," Lucas explained.

"That's a good idea," Tony responded.

As they left the science center, they heard a voice. It sounded like Sulieman. It was coming from a small room nearby. They looked in. Sulieman was kneeling on a prayer rug, praying.

"Do you want to fill him in?" Lucas asked.

Tony struggled with the question. He felt he could trust Sulieman, he just didn't know if getting him involved was the right thing to do.

"If we tell him, he has to come with us. I don't want this news getting out. Most of the crew doesn't even know yet. The captain feels that the more people who know, the harder it will be to maintain the 'business as usual' façade. Let him finish, then we'll tell him. Prayer is important; and we need all the help we can get."

When Sulieman finished with his prayers, Lucas and Tony approached.

"Can we talk to you?"

"Sure."

"You got any plans this evening? We need some help."

"No specific plans. I can help. What's up?"

Lucas looked around to make sure no one was nearby. "The following conversation stays between us, and only us. At least for now. Agreed?"

Sulieman looked confused and concerned. "Sure," he said slowly.

"We have a killer on board. A cabin steward was found strangled to death. We're going to check out the area where she was found. Now that you know, you need to stay with us. Ok?"

Sulieman was visibly upset. "Ok."

When they got to Lucia's area, they saw an older couple headed to their cabin, room 208. When they paused to unlock their door, Lucas approached them. "Hey, do you guys like this hallway? Is it quiet? I've got noisy neighbors. They're driving me nuts."

The couple looked at Lucas with uncertainty. He was still carrying the bottle of beer he brought with him.

Tony interjected, "Sorry folks. I'm Tony, the ship's purser. This guy's been complaining about his neighbors. Give him a couple of beers and now he wants to walk around the ship, looking for a quieter hallway."

"Well," the woman said, "If you can get the people in 204 to switch with him, I wouldn't mind. Yesterday there were people going in and out constantly, at all hours. It was like party central. Earlier I heard a scream, and I was sure it came from that room."

"Did you tell anybody about this, Ma'am?"

"Oh yes. We told a crew member on the main deck. A nice gentleman, but he seemed a bit preoccupied. We would have told our cleaning lady, but she never came to clean our room. I hope she's okay. Such a sweet girl. They had to send someone else to do it."

"I want to look into this and make sure the crew member you told followed the proper procedures. Can you describe him?"

The couple provided a description. About 5'10", dark olive skin, medium build, black hair and a moustache. "His name tag said Ramez," the husband added.

"I hear movement and noises in there," the woman added, "even when it seems no one is in there. I think they smuggled an animal on board. Although I can't imagine why."

"Thanks. We'll check it out."

Now they had a very suspicious cabin and a valid reason to enter it. Tony knocked on the door of 204. "Ship's purser. Hello? Anybody there?"

The woman they had spoken to lingered in the hallway, waiting to see if someone opened the door.

"Come on dear," her husband encouraged. "Let them do their job. We don't need to be a part of this." They both disappeared into their room.

The men heard movement inside of room 204, but no voices. The woman was right. Something was in that room. Something alive.

Tony spoke again. "Ship's purser. I apologize for intruding but if anybody is in there, I need to make sure you're okay. I'm coming in."

A noise came from the other side of the door. It sounded like a growl.

The men looked at each other. *What the hell?*

Tony turned his head to look down the hall in both directions to confirm there was no one in the hallway. He took a deep breath and opened the door. Something alive was in the room.

A woman.

Gagged and tied to a chair.

Chapter 8:

Tosin in Tripoli

At first Tosin spent most of his time with Samir and Eman. They said it was best to not overwhelm him. They began teaching him about the world, about Tripoli and the Muslim religion. He spent his days at the mosque, learning the significance of everything in it. He was given assignments and chores.

One day Eman said to Tosin "We're going out today. Just the two of us."

Tosin had only been at the mosque for a few weeks. He hadn't done much except his chores and assignments. The only time he left the mosque was to go home with Eman or Samir.

"Where are we going?"

"It's a surprise."

Tosin understood the meaning of a surprise, but he had never experienced a pleasant one. Eman's smile told him that it was a good surprise. Tosin was excited. He knew he was going to learn something new. Outside of the mosque walls.

It was a beautiful day. They set out on their adventure. After they had been walking for several minutes Tosin asked, "How far are we walking?"

"Not far."

They walked in silence for a few more minutes. Tosin was taking in everything that he could see. He hadn't seen this much of the city since he arrived. It wasn't nearly as scary in the daylight. They were walking mostly between buildings. It felt a bit dark and cramped, but Tosin didn't mind. Eman seemed to have chosen this path for a reason. They slowed down and Tosin asked again, "Now may I know where we are going?"

Eman stepped forward, motioning for Tosin to stay where he was. Eman looked to his left. Tosin couldn't see what he was looking at. Then Eman held out his hand and said, "The ocean."

Tosin took his hand and stepped forward. He looked in the direction that Eman had. There it was. For the first time in his life, he was looking at the ocean. The actual ocean.

"Can we go to the water?"

"Yes. Would you like to run?"

"Yes." Together they ran to the water. Tosin hadn't felt that free in his entire life. He had gained some weight over the past few weeks and had gotten stronger. He felt like he could run for miles. The clothes that he got that were too big for him when he arrived now almost fit him.

Tosin stopped before his feet touched the water. He looked to the horizon, as far as he could see. It was so massive.

"It's okay," Eman said. "You don't have to go in if you don't want to. I'm right here if you do."

Tosin nodded. He needed to do this. He wanted to do this.

Eman went in so the water was just above his knees. He motioned to Tosin. "Come in when you're ready. I'm right here."

Tosin took a tentative step forward. The water tickled his toes. He looked down at the water, then back up to Eman. Eman held out both of his hands. "Just walk to me. Take your time."

Tosin continued until he reached Eman. "Look," Eman said, pointing down.

Tosin looked into the water and saw lots of little fish swimming around. He gasped. "Fish! There's so many."

Tosin wanted to see more. His apprehension evaporated in an instant. "Can I go under the water?"

"Yes."

"Can I open my eyes under water?"

"Yes, but only for a few seconds. It may make your eyes sting. The ocean is salt water. Try not to drink it. It will make you very thirsty. Would you like to hold my hand?"

Tosin nodded.

"Take a deep breath and hold it. Then go under and take a look. I got you."

Tosin was completely mesmerized. He saw the fish dart away when he invaded their space. He wanted to follow them. He had barely begun learning about the land that he lived on. Now he wanted to learn about the water too.

Tosin spent just over three years at the mosque, learning about the Muslim religion and the world he lived in. He went to primary school and had a strict daily schedule of chores, assignments and prayer. Eventually he was able to spend time with different members of the mosque and their families. Each member taking him into their home for a certain amount of time. Each household was different. All with very similar beliefs, but different ways of acting on their beliefs. There were so many ways to look at the world. At first Tosin was confused. Eventually he decided that maybe there just isn't one right way to do anything. Everyone has a different way;, and they each believe that their way is the only way.

There was one family that was Tosin's favorite. The Sulimans. They had three kids. Saif was the oldest. Nidal was Tosin's age. He was the middle child. Suha was the youngest. The only girl, and the apple of her father's eye. Their parents, Imad and Imas, were kind and welcoming.

Tosin and Nidal spent most of their free time together at school and whenever Tosin stayed with them. As the boys became best friends, Tosin would spend longer periods of time at their house. Whenever it was time for Tosin to leave and stay elsewhere, Nidal would always complain and beg his parents to let him stay. When the boys entered secondary school at age sixteen, Tosin was invited to live with the Sulimans full time. Saif had graduated from secondary school and moved out. Tosin got his own room.

As the boys got older, they pushed past the boundaries that had been set for them. They took longer to come home from school, taking different routes through areas that they had never been to before. If they got any freedom in the city, without the watchful eye of Nidal's parents, they would take off and explore. Tosin had never had a best friend before. He never had the luxury of being carefree. There was so much to see and do – and eat. The city seemed magical to him. Like a huge treasure chest full of precious items to be discovered. He wanted to see it all, do it all and eat it all. Tosin loved food. Years after escaping his village, he still feared starvation. He was getting tall, and at the dinner table, he usually ate more than anybody else.

Tosin wanted to get a job. The lure of the city was becoming irresistible. He was nearly eighteen and almost done with secondary school. He wanted his own money to buy what he wanted and do what he wanted. Nidal's parents said no.

"The city isn't safe. Wait until you finish secondary school, then you can get a respectable and safe job," they said.

Since he now lived there permanently, they were the closest thing to parents that he had. Tosin didn't want a 'safe' job. He wasn't ready for a mind-numbing, boring adult job. He needed new, exciting and amazing experiences. He needed to *live*. He went to the mosque and tried to convince Samir that it was a good idea. Samir said no too.

"I agree with Imad and Imas. Wait until you finish school."

Eman was off on a mission trip. Tosin had only seen Eman a few times over the past year. He missed him. Eman would understand and let me get a job. He earned some money doing odd jobs, but it wasn't enough. He wanted more.

Tosin would see people in the city wearing bright colors and sparkling jewelry. He wanted to wear those things. He saw groups of young people that would hang out together every day, laughing. They looked carefree. He had felt invisible his whole life. He wanted to be seen. He wanted to be heard. He wanted to belong.

Tosin's wardrobe had been mundane and boring since he arrived in Tripoli. The clothes he was given when he arrived were the most luxurious things he'd ever worn. Now he was older. He should have a say in what he wears.

On days when the family was in the city together, Tosin would admire the clothing and jewelry that he couldn't have. Imad would say to him, "You don't want to wear any of that. You don't want to be noticed here. It's not safe. Best to blend in. It will keep you out of trouble." All Tosin heard was Stay invisible. Be boring.

One day after school Tosin convinced Nidal to take a detour to the area where the shops were. They had never gone into the shopping district on their own. Nidal protested. "It's not safe. My parents said never to go there without them."

"It's where people shop. How dangerous can it be? Don't you like looking at all the amazing stuff for sale?"

"All the stuff I can't have? Not really."

"Fine. I'll go by myself. Just cover for me with your parents. Make something up."

Nidal sighed. "I'm coming too. We're not staying long."

Tosin could have spent hours browsing through the shops. This much merchandise still amazed him.

This is what I escaped the village for, he thought. A chance to have what everyone else has.

Tosin had a particular item in mind. He went straight to the shop with the shirt in it that had caught his eye days earlier. It was a button up shirt with a collar. It was soft and loose fitting with bright colors. It demanded attention. Tosin hadn't been able to get the shirt out of his mind. He checked the price tag. He didn't have enough money to buy it. "Do you have any money on you?" he asked Nidal.

"No. My parents told me not to carry money. A lot of muggings happen here. They told you that too."

"So how do all of these people buy stuff if they don't have money?"

"I guess they hope they don't get mugged."

Tosin had the shirt in his hands. He was admiring it, making sure it was the right size. He should just put it back. Go home and save up his money. It was just a shirt. He hadn't planned what happened next. He didn't know what compelled him to do it. He shoved the shirt in his school bag and quickly walked away.

"Are you crazy? Tosin, we will both get arrested!"

"Just walk. Fast."

Nidal had no choice but to try to keep up with Tosin as they left the shopping district.

They didn't get far. Just outside of the shopping district, they were approached by a group of young men who blocked their path.

"Nice lift. That's a nice shirt you stole. Let me see it." The man speaking stood at the front of the group. Four men behind him were looking on, sneering.

"I don't know what you're talking about. Please move. We need to get home."

"Listen kid, I'm going to see that shirt. Either you take it out of your bag and hand it to me or I take the bag from you. If I have to take the bag from you, it will not end well for you and your friend."

Tosin looked at Nidal. Nidal was pale and terrified. Was this a gang? An actual gang? Tosin's heart sank. *What have I done?* He pulled the shirt out of the bag and tossed it to the man. "Here, keep it. Just let us go."

The man held the shirt up. "This isn't my size. It's too small. You're going to go get me a bigger one."

"I can't go steal another one. The shop owner will grab me as soon as I show my face."

"Well, you're going to have to." Two men from the group walked up and grabbed Nidal by each arm. "Cuz we're going to keep your friend here until you come back with my shirt."

"I need him to distract the shop owner. There's no way I'm going to get away with it again by myself."

"Dragon here will go with you. Get going. I ain't got all day."

Tosin and Dragon headed back to the shops. Tosin was shaking and furious with himself. *What the hell were you thinking? You put Nidal in danger and no one knows where we are.* "Is Dragon your gang name?" he asked.

"Yep. I'll distract the owner; you get the shirt. Don't try to make a run for it. Your friend will suffer greatly if you do. Blade is not very forgiving."

After the deed was done, Tosin threw the shirt at Blade. "Here, I did what you asked. Now let us go."

"I don't think so. You're pretty handy. You've got some skills, and your face isn't well known around here."

"Nidal!" It was Imas, calling for her son. She had come looking for them.

"That's my mom. Let us go."

Blade motioned his head to Nidal, then out toward the sound of Imas's voice. The gang members pulled Nidal to the side of the building and shoved him out into the open.

"Nidal!" Imas exclaimed. She had found her son. "Where's Tosin?" she asked.

Tosin took a step forward. Blade grabbed his arm.

"Not you. I'm keeping you. Welcome to the Bloody Knives."

At twelve years old, Tosin left everything he had ever known for a chance at a better life. At seventeen, he lost everything due to his stupidity and selfishness.

Chapter 9:

The Bloody Knives

The initiation ceremony into the Bloody Knives was a severe beating. Each of the five members getting to beat Tosin while thoroughly enjoying the task. Blade, of course, delivered the worst of it. That was his right as head of the gang. It was the first step in breaking him. Next came captivity, starvation, lack of water and constant threats. He was locked in a room for three days with minimal food and water. Locked in for three days. This is familiar. He had to urinate and defecate in the room, and he had to clean it all up when he was finally set free. Blade needed to make sure Tosin would be compliant. When he was convinced that Tosin would do what he asked without question, Tosin joined them on the streets.

The next step was to get Tosin to stay. There are different ways to accomplish this. Sometimes it takes more threats and violence. Sometimes acting like their best friend does the trick. Blade chose the latter option first. It's always more enjoyable. Beating people up is a lot of work. And it hurts his hands.

After being released, Tosin got a formal introduction to his new 'family'. Blade made the introductions. "This is Lefty." Lefty stepped forward and swung at Tosin with his left fist. When Tosin reacted, Lefty quickly landed a punch to Tosin's gut with his right. They all laughed.

Blade continued, "He's not called Lefty because he's left-handed, but he's great at pretending he is. We call him Lefty because that makes people think he's left-handed. It gives him an advantage. People are always surprised when he pummels them with his right hand. Never gets old. Next up is Pyro."

Pyro gave his own explanation, "I like fire. I wanted to be called Blaze, but it sounds too much like Blade. Pyro works just fine."

"You already know Dragon. And this big guy," Blade continued, "is Mighty Mac. We just call him Mac."

"'Sup?" Mac grunted. Apparently, Mac is a man of few words.

On his first night on the streets with them, Tosin was treated like the most important member of the gang. They ate out and Tosin got to eat whatever he wanted. He ate all of his food, and everything left over that the rest of the gang didn't finish. Tosin wore the shirt he had stolen. The gang members kept telling him how great he looked in that shirt. Even Blade complimented him and acted impressed. They took him to a tattoo shop where he got the same tattoo the rest of them had. A bloody dagger, with blood dripping from the tip. Since Blade felt keeping the gang inconspicuous was important, he allowed the tattoo to be applied on the shoulder, where it could be covered. Many gangs had their tattoos on their hands or faces, to be worn like a badge of honor for all to see and fear. Blade even showed him his prized possession; a dagger called a Tebu arm knife. "It's been in my family for generations," Blade had told him. "I stole it from my dad when I left home. I figured I was going to need it more than he did." Blade spun the dagger around, twirling the handle around his finger. Tosin watched the dagger spin with a sense of awe and admiration. Blade instantaneously grabbed the handle and lashed at Tosin's neck, blade facing out, just missing his jugular. "Knives are my weapon of choice. I'm pretty good with them. Most people prefer guns. Guns are for lazy people with no imagination." Blade had made it perfectly clear how easily he could end a life. Tosin got the message.

Step three: Convince Tosin that the Suliman's had abandoned him. They didn't want him around. If they did, they would have tried harder to get him back. They hadn't even bothered to continue looking for him. They just went about their lives, happy to be rid of him. Tosin had no way of knowing if this was true, but once the Bloody Knives had his trust, it was easier to sell the story. Which leads to step four.

Step four: Convince Tosin that the Bloody Knives are the only people he can count on. "We got your back. All of us.", Blade would say. "We won't abandon you when things get rough. Just don't cross me, or I'll have to teach you a lesson."

Step five: Tell Tosin about the money he can make staying with the Bloody Knives; and prove it.

One of Blade's rules was no drug use. He had thrown members out of the gang for using. He didn't want to have to take care of a bunch of addicts. Besides, addicts were useless. All they cared about was getting their next high. Dealing drugs was good money. The Bloody Knives did not deal drugs. At least they didn't sell it on the street. There was too much competition and too much risk. Crossing the wrong drug dealer will get you killed. Allowing your gang to be known as drug dealers makes you a target. Blade wasn't willing to die over a bag of coke. Occasionally however, he would wedge the Bloody Knives into the supply chain if the conditions were right and the payoff was big enough. Jobs like that didn't come along often. When they did it was usually because of a major upheaval in the supply chain. Once an opportunity presented itself when all of the members of a gang were arrested. This put a stop to their daily drug dealing activities. Blade knew another gang would quickly take over. There might even be a turf war if more than one gang wanted to acquire the stalled merchandise and claim the newly abandoned clientele. Blade wanted no part of that. The Bloody Knives stepped in to move the drugs and get them 'unstuck'.

Got paid handsomely for it too. Then they laid low for a while and let the gangs fight it out while the bodies piled up. The same opportunity came around again after another gang eliminated itself by killing each other. There had been a fight for leadership. The leader lost, but certain members of the gang didn't want the winner to be the leader. So, they killed him. And so on. And so on. And so on. Until there was only one guy left. That guy disappeared. People think he saw his opportunity for a better life and took it. Probably took a fortune with him too. No one knows what happened to the cash that must have been hidden somewhere.

Keeping the Bloody Knives out of the mainstream gang activity had worked out well. With only five members, now six, they had no hope of competing with any major gang. They also had no hope of surviving if they pissed off one of those gangs. Blade had built a reputation. The Bloody Knives were known as the gang that stayed out of your business. If you needed a small group to help you out of a jam, come talk to him. They always delivered as promised and had never double-crossed any of the other gangs. This earned them respect. The larger gangs recognized their value and left them alone. More than once, a smaller gang tried to take over the Bloody Knives' position in the city. The larger gangs eliminated them. Every time. With respect comes protection.

Blade had to be very selective about the jobs he took. He had to be sure that their actions wouldn't anger any of the large gangs, but he could never be absolutely sure. He did his best to confirm the facts and make sure he wasn't being lied to. That happened once. He took a job. Turned out the Bloody Knives were being used for interference so one gang could try to take out another. Blade figured it out and aborted. His gang went into hiding while the two gangs settled their differences by killing each other.

Blade got a simple drug-moving job just when he needed it. He needed the first job with Tosin on the team to be an easy one. The first job with a new member is a big risk. If Tosin screwed up, he could ruin the gang's reputation. Without the respect and protection of the larger gangs, the Bloody Knives wouldn't last a week. They'd have to leave Tripoli just to survive.

The first job was simply to go to the docks, pick up a drug shipment arriving by boat and deliver it to the specified location. They weren't dealing directly with the supplier. They weren't dealing directly with the gangs. They were dealing with a middleman who needed a delivery service. No one could fault them for that.

Blade addressed his guys before they left for the docks. "Remember, this must go exactly as planned. If we screw up, it's our necks. As always, don't even think about taking any of the drugs. If even one ounce is missing, they'll come after us. We do what we promise and don't double-cross anybody. That's how we stay alive."

Tosin wondered why they weren't going to keep the drugs. *If we kept the drugs, we could make a fortune*. He didn't say anything. He knew better than to question Blade. They did the job exactly as planned. Tosin thought about keeping some of the drugs for himself, but decided he wasn't willing to accept the consequences. He did his job exactly as instructed. He got paid well too. Blade had asked for a larger fee for this job. He wanted to make sure that Tosin's share would be big enough to entice him to stay.

Tosin spent his eighteenth birthday with the Bloody Knives. He didn't tell any of them that it was his birthday. He hadn't been with the gang long enough to know what would happen. He just acted like it was any other ordinary day. He remembered his first birthday in Tripoli. His thirteenth birthday. It was his first birthday party, and he was the guest of honor. There was singing and food and sweets and presents. It was very overwhelming. He wondered if anyone thought about him today. Did Eman or Nidal or Mrs. Suliman think about him today, on his birthday? Did his mother think about him today? Was she even alive? Tosin liked to imagine that his absence had made her life a little easier. That she had gained a little weight and was fine. He prayed that she hadn't had any more children. That was one thing she did not need.

Another year went by. Tosin learned that birthdays were recognized in the Bloody Knives. There was no party, no singing, no sweets. Usually all you got was a punch in the arm and an uncomfortable off-the-cuff comment about getting old. If a birthday happened to coincide with a job that they had been paid well for, Blade would let them splurge a bit. They would eat better and drink more. Tosin managed to avoid a nineteenth birthday celebration. That was on purpose. By the time Dragon asked, "Hey, when's your birthday?" Tosin just shrugged and said his birthday had already passed. He really didn't want a punch in the arm. No one ever asked about it again.

Tosin hadn't seen the Sulimans since the day he stole the shirt and ended up with the Bloody Knives. He avoided that shopping area. He stayed away on purpose. He was ashamed of who he was and afraid of what they would think of him. He didn't want anyone to be able to make a connection between him and the Sulimans. No one from the Bloody Knives saw Imas's face that night. He wanted to keep it that way. He knew Nidal would be graduated by now and has probably moved away to start his adult life. Tosin found it ironic that the day he stole the shirt, he thought an adult life would be unbearably boring. Now he thought it sounded wonderful.

Being a well-behaved team member had earned Tosin some freedom. He was able to move about the city as he pleased, as long as he followed Blade's instructions. Rule #1 was never interact with any of the other gangs. Rule #2 was keep your head down and stay invisible. Invisible. Invisible is good. He wished he had known that before he stole the shirt. He wished he had listened to Imad.

On most days when he had some free time he went to the ocean. It was calm and peaceful, and the gangs didn't hang out there. In his mind he replayed the day he first saw the ocean with Eman. He replayed that day every time he went there. Every single time. He had stayed away from the mosque for the same reasons he stayed away from the Sulimans. There was no place for him there. How could he expect Allah to forgive him if he couldn't forgive himself?

After staring at the ocean for what seemed like hours, he started to walk back to the gang hangout.

"Tosin, is that you?" Tosin froze. He didn't recognize the voice. He wished he was invisible. He turned his head. It was Suha, Nidal's little sister. She wasn't little anymore. She was all grown up. She was beautiful.

As soon as she saw Tosin's face, her face lit up – like he was the most beautiful thing she had ever seen. No one had ever looked at Tosin like that before. Not ever. She ran up to him and threw her arms around his neck. She had to stand on her tiptoes to do it.

"I'm so happy to see you!" she started talking fast. "Tosin, I'm so sorry. Mom and Dad came looking for you that night. The night we lost you. Mom was by herself when she found Nidal. Dad wasn't home yet. Nidal told her there was a gang. They rushed home to get Dad. He was there by the time they got back. They came back immediately to get you, but they couldn't find you. Mom cried for days. I don't think Nidal ever got over losing you. He was never himself after that. We've been trying to find you ever since."

Tosin just nodded, trying to process it all. Part of him wanted to believe her. The Sulimans were good people. They wouldn't have abandoned him. They would have at least tried. But there was a part of him that had hardened. The part that goes numb when you just can't take being hurt anymore. That part was winning.

He gently pulled her arms from around his neck. "Thanks. I've gotten involved in some bad stuff with some terrible people. You can't be seen with me. You need to forget you ever saw me and never tell anybody. They'll hurt you and your family." He started to walk away.

Suha followed, trying to keep up with his long strides. "You're our family. You have been since the first time you stayed at our house. That's why Mom and Dad decided you should live with us full time. You belong with us." Suha was getting angry. The Sulimans had claimed Tosin as their own and someone had taken him away from them. She continued, "I'll be graduating soon. I've been studying finance, and I have a good chance at getting a job at The Libyan Bank. I want you to be there when I graduate. Saif isn't going to make it, but Nidal will be there. Tosin, I can't keep this from Nidal and my parents. They miss you so much."

"Suha, you don't know what I know. Trust me on this. My stupidity got me into this mess. Don't let your stupidity get your family killed."

Suha looked hurt, as if Tosin had just stabbed her in the chest. Her dark eyes were sad, but still beautiful. Tosin felt dizzy just looking at them. He steeled himself and glared at her, "Just go."

She backed away, still looking at him. Then she turned and ran off. Tosin knew he had hurt her. This was the closest thing to being loved that he had ever experienced. He didn't know how to process that. He hated hurting her. She didn't deserve it, but it had to be done. He continued on his way, hoping his exchange with Suha hadn't attracted the wrong kind of attention.

Tosin couldn't think straight after his encounter with Suha. Every day after that he waited for his life to get worse than it already was. He expected to see one of the Sulimans and they would tell him what a terrible person he was for hurting Suha. How he was no longer welcome in the family. Worse than that, every day he expected to find out that the gangs in the city had discovered his connection to them. He knew the gangs would take advantage of that. They would use the family to control him. He couldn't let that happen.

He was at Suha's graduation, but she didn't know it. He stayed out of sight and didn't talk to anybody. She had asked him to be there. That meant a lot to him. It was good seeing the family together. Seeing them happy. It was a memory he could take with him. One he could cherish. The next day he got on a ferry headed to Malta. He left Tripoli behind forever.

Chapter 10:

Laying Low

In room 204, Tony rushed to the captive woman. "Don't make a sound. No one can know we found you." He removed the gag. "Tosin!" she whispered loudly. As loud as she dared.

Lucas and Tony looked at Sulieman, questioning. "Tosin?" they said in unison.

The woman started speaking frantically. "I'm so happy to see you. I have been so scared. These people are terrible. Tosin, please tell me you're not part of this. You can't be. You just can't."

Lucas looked at Tosin. "I'm guessing there's more to the story."

"Guys, this is Suha. Suha, meet Lucas and Tony."

"*You're* Lucas and Tony? I overheard them talking about you two. They say you're a couple of do-gooders that are going to get in their way."

"In the way of what?" Tony asked. "We don't even know what's going on. Besides, it's my job."

Suha looked at Tosin. "You're here with the good guys. Please tell me you're not going to go along with the gang."

"I left Tripoli to get away from the gangs and keep you safe. I didn't know you were onboard. They kidnapped you? Why? Have they hurt you?"

"They said I'm a twofer. They can use me as a hostage, and they can use me because I work for the bank. I have no idea what they expect to get from me. They snatched me from work a few days ago. They haven't hurt me, except push me around and threaten to kill me every chance they get. I know Mom and Dad are sick with worry. I hope they're okay."

"They're okay. The gang will use your disappearance to keep them in line. They won't be harmed as long as they can be controlled. You won't be harmed as long as they need you."

"You know a lot about this," Tony said.

"Yeah, I was in a gang for over a year. Not by choice. I was basically kidnapped. It was a small one. We stayed away from the major gangs. Kept to ourselves. The gangs in Tripoli have a lot of money, a lot of power and a lot of control. I have no doubt they are deeply engrained with the bank." He looked at Suha," Where do Saif and Nadil work?"

"Saif moved to the Zawiya District. He works in IT. Nadil works for the Libyan Oil Corporation."

Lucas and Tony looked at Tosin, questioning.

"Saif and Nadil are Suha's brothers. Their parents took me in and made me a part of their family. It's a long story," Tosin responded.

"Are the gangs engrained in the oil company too?" Lucas asked.

"I'm sure they are."

"So, what is your name?"

"Tosin Manko is the name I was given at birth. I left Tripoli and fled to Malta under the name Sulieman Aremu."

"Sulieman," Suha said softly, smiling. She was looking at Tosin with the same loving gaze he had seen when they met unexpectedly in Tripoli. He liked that look, but he didn't feel he deserved it. When he had contacted someone in Tripoli for a fake ID, he had asked for that first name. Suha knew why.

"Was the cabin steward killed in this room?" Tony asked.

"The cleaning lady? Yes, it was awful." Suha began shaking, choking back tears. "There was one person in this room, Moose. He was sleeping. The cleaning lady knocked on the door. He didn't respond and I certainly couldn't. He woke up when she walked in. How she didn't hear his snoring through the door is a mystery. She screamed when she saw me here, like this. Moose grabbed her. I closed my eyes. I couldn't watch. I could hear her struggling. Then nothing. I didn't open my eyes until I heard the door close. When I did, Moose, the cleaning lady and her cart were all gone. I was alone."

"So technically you didn't see him kill her."

"No, but I know he did."

Tony started to untie Suha. "Tony, we can't," Lucas said.

Tony gave Lucas an incredulous look. "We can't leave her here."

"We have to. They'll know."

"Lucas is right," Tosin said. "If we take her with us, there will be no reason for whoever is involved to remain in hiding. They'll kill everyone that they don't need. It will be a bloodbath."

"They'll kill her as soon as they realize we're onto them," Tony protested.

"No, they won't. They'll use her as a bargaining chip, but they will kill passengers. We need a plan first."

"Tosin don't leave me here, please. I hate it here. I hate them. You don't know what it's like. Please!"

Tosin walked to Suha, kissed her forehead and knelt in front of her. "I do know what it's like. I'm sorry. It has to be this way. At least until I know I can keep you safe."

Suha looked at the floor, then met Tosin's gaze. Tears streamed down her cheeks. Tosin hated seeing her like this.

"I know you know what it's like," Suha said. "When I was younger, I heard Mom and Dad talking about how you came to Tripoli. Three days in the back of a truck, alone and scared. I can't even imagine what you've been through. I trust you. I'll stay. But Tosin, I don't know how long I can hold myself together. You have to get me out of here. Soon."

"It's the first thing on my list. I promise."

Tony spoke. "We need to go. We've been here long enough. Suha, you need to stay quiet. A couple in a nearby cabin reported the noises coming from here. I'm going to tell them it's been taken care of and make up a reason that they shouldn't mention it to any crew members again. They can't keep hearing noises from this cabin."

"Ok. Oh, I heard Moose say they were going to poison the food the morning we arrive. I don't know if the poison will kill everybody or just knock them out. I don't have any other details. Moose got reprimanded just for saying that in front of me. They want the ship to get there before they make their move."

"Thanks. That's a big help. Did you hear anything else about their plan?"

"No. Moose thought I was asleep when he said that."

The look on Suha's face as the men left her in the cabin tore Tosin's heart out. He hated leaving her there. She didn't deserve this, but it had to be done.

Chapter 11:

The Bridge

Once Lucas, Tony, and Tosin knew it was safe to talk, Lucas looked at Tosin. "You need to tell us what you know."

"There's a Libyan gang on board, at least part of one. I recognized some gang members from Tripoli and figured they weren't here for vacation. I followed them. I know where their weapons are."

"Can you get us there without being caught?"

"I think so."

"Let's go. Tell us everything you know on the way."

They walked to the lowest level on the ship. Tosin told them everything he knew. He told them about being a member of the Bloody Knives, and how he was recruited. He knew the three new crew members were the ones who smuggled the weapons onto the ship. He heard them say other gang members had been hired on as crew as well, but he didn't know who or how many. "It has something to do with oil under the ocean," he told them. "They want to control the land there, so they have access to that part of the ocean."

"So Nadil could be a part of this?"

"He's not part of the gang, I am sure of that. But they could use him the same way they're using Suha."

Antarctica's first major turf war. Lucas's mind was reeling. With enough soldiers and weapons, it was possible to take over any of the bases on the continent, and the land that goes with it. Who's going to stop them? Antarctica doesn't belong to anybody. It has no government and no military.

"I've been praying to Allah for guidance to help me stop this. I want no part of this, and now they have Suha."

They walked quietly. Being careful not to raise suspicion. "They're in these," Tosin said, pointing to crates marked as supplies. "I don't know which crates. Some are what it says on the box. I'm guessing they would have put the weapons in the back, hoping nobody opened them. I'm pretty sure they stashed some in with the laundry supplies too."

Lucas and Tony took a minute to pull a couple of crates from the back and check. There were guns and grenades and lots of other stuff. There were weapons in there that Lucas didn't even know what they did, and he didn't want to find out.

Lucas looked around and found the most inconspicuous bags he could. He emptied the contents and put some of the guns and grenades in them. He rearranged the remaining weapons around so you couldn't tell anything was missing unless you moved the contents.

Thoughts were forming in Lucas's head so fast he could barely sort through them to start a plan. "Tony, we need everything you can get on the crew. We need to figure out who may be in on this. They could be mixed in with the dining staff, the stewards, maintenance. They could be everywhere. We need to know who we can trust."

"I know some that have been working for this cruise line for years."

"Good. Write down every crew member on this ship that you know can be trusted."

"Got it. I've got to talk to the captain," Tony said. "I need to know what he knows and vice versa."

"Do you trust him?"

"Yes. I hope he's still in charge. Are you guys coming?"

"No," Lucas said. "The three of us sticking together like the Three Musketeers might raise suspicion. How about we meet at the bridge in half an hour?"

"Sounds good," Tosin said. "I need to go back to get my prayer rug. Hope it's still there."

Back in his cabin, Lucas emptied his backpack and put the weapons in. He covered them up with a towel. He headed to the bridge with a bag that was packing some heat. He decided to eat a banana on the way, nodding hello to everyone he passed. Maybe that would make him look less suspicious.

When he got to the bridge he was let in right away. He joined Tony and Tosin, who were already there.

"Welcome to the bridge Mr. Kalloe. I'm Captain Grayson. Tony speaks highly of you."

Lucas shook his hand. "Thanks. This is a nice ship you've got here." He was going to keep it cordial until he knew it was safe.

"Yes, and I intend to keep it that way."

Tony looked at Lucas. "You already know Sulieman."

Tosin is keeping his cover. Got it., Lucas thought.

There were six people on the bridge. Captain Grayson, two other bridge officers, Lucas, Tony and Tosin. A crew member entered the bridge. "Sir, there's an issue in the engine room."

"Is it an emergency?"

"No sir, but the engine room staff has asked for somebody to come down there. I was told to inform you."

"Ed, would you go to the engine room and check it out?"

"Sure."

Once Ed and the crew member had left the bridge, the captain spoke. "I haven't known Ed long enough to know that I can trust him." He motioned to the other officer. "This is Jack, my First Officer. I've known him for over ten years. I trust him."

"We've both confirmed our families are safe," Jack added. "We didn't want that to become an issue."

Lucas reached into his backpack and pulled out the weapons. "First things first. You need to know I got these."

"Under normal circumstances those would never be allowed on the bridge, but these aren't normal circumstances," Captain Grayson said. "Jack and I have access to our own. A perk of being the two highest officers on the ship. Tony has filled me in on what you found in 204. Let us know if you need help getting that rectified as soon as possible."

"Have you been able to contact anybody regarding our situation?"

"Yes. This ship wasn't built for cloak and dagger operations, but we do have a few options at our disposal. I am confident we were able to get the word out without raising suspicion. We've received responses from some of the ships that are leaving the bases for the winter. They are now standing by waiting to assist. There is no one close enough to come to our aid immediately. They will be at the continent when we arrive. There are several countries who do not want to see a major turf war there. They won't stand for it. I won't stand for it."

The captain continued, "If this really is about the oil deposits in the Weddell Sea, they're probably going after control of the Antarctic Peninsula. There are lots of bases there they can use to set up operations. My question is, are they doing this to claim the land for the Libyan government?"

"The Libyan government could be involved," Tosin explained. "The government has been fractured for over a decade. It's broke. It has no money and no real power. There's bickering and constant uprisings over who should have control. People who claim to be government leaders are now directing organized crime to get what they want. That's one of the reasons the gangs have been able to gain so much power. They're not even gangs anymore. They're businesses. They make millions while the citizens fight for scraps. Their employees are loyal and well-trained. I can almost guarantee you that Russia is involved. Russia is very much involved with the Libyan government, and they're the ones who discovered the oil deposits."

"And Captain," Tosin continued, "our allies need to act as normal as possible if we do make it to the continent. There may be ships there that aren't on our side. They'll attack if they think they're being threatened."

"Sulieman lived in Tripoli. He knows a lot about organized crime there," Lucas explained.

The captain nodded. "We're talking over 500 billion gallons of oil. They can't even think about drilling for it until they control the land. If that's their plan, they have one hell of a fight ahead of them."

"So do we."

"They'll destroy everything there to get what they want," Jack said.

"Governments won't let that happen."

Tosin spoke up. "Won't they? They didn't bother to stop the slaughter of rhinos for profit."

Everyone looked at him for an explanation.

"The western black rhino is now considered extinct. They used to roam the plains in the country I was born in. The last one was seen in 2006. *2006.*" He repeated the date to make his point clear. "We could've stopped it. Governments could have stopped it. People could have stopped it. We didn't, because there wasn't any profit in saving them. And now they're gone." Tosin paused then continued. "The northern white rhino is considered functionally extinct. There are an estimated less than 100 Javan rhinos in existence. They are all in Indonesia. Same with the Sumatran rhino. Less than 100."

"This is different."

"Is it? Maybe. Should it be? No." Tosin was agitated. "Rhinos are still slaughtered every day. There's more than one species. They exterminate one species and just move on to the next most profitable option. They'll keep being slaughtered until there are none left. You know what's even worse? They're killed only for their horns, for profit. There's not one documented case of rhino horns saving a human life, or any life. Not that I've ever found. We wiped out an entire species for nothing. *Nothing.* Am I the only one seeing a pattern here? The ice can't defend itself. The penguins and seals can't pay people to fight for them. Just like the rhinos can't. The money lies at the bottom of the ocean, so that's all anybody is going to care about. You know I'm right."

Silence. No one could argue with him. It was hard to admit, but he was right.

Finally, Tony spoke, "We have to stop this. And we still don't know what their plan is."

They talked as long as they could about the details of the situation. They had more questions than answers, but the captain, Jack and Tony provided a lot of information about the ship and how it worked. Electronics, communications, the engine, the food. They tried to cover everything they could think of.

Tony pulled a piece of paper out of his pocket. "I wrote down the names of everyone I think we can trust. The captain has reviewed it, and he agrees. Tosin added names and descriptions of everyone that he knows of that is part of the gang." Tony continued. "Take a picture of these with your phones. I plan on destroying the list. I also have master key cards. These will get you into most rooms on the ship, including cabins. To be clear, you cannot start barging into cabins. Keep it calm and professional."

"Can these be reprogrammed?"

"Yes, but reprogramming ours won't do much good. We need the ones that they have."

"Did you put George and Grace on the list?" Lucas asked.

"No," Tony smiled, getting the joke. "June isn't on the list either. I didn't include passengers. June, George and Grace are considered trustworthy."

"Are George and Grace the penguins?" the captain asked.

"Yes," Lucas and Tony answered in unison.

"I will talk to everyone we can trust," Tony said. "I know who they are."

"Get yourself a partner, Tony," the captain said. "I don't want anybody moving around on the ship alone. Jack and I are going to stay right here until all of this is over. It's imperative we keep the bridge secure. Sulieman, do you think they'll try to take the ship?"

"If we're right, the ship is going right where they want it to go. There's no reason to try to take control before we reach the continent. Once we're there, they will try to take it. It's too valuable. It gives them food and supplies. With enough soldiers and weapons, they can turn it into a battleship. Their first line of defense. They won't think twice about killing everybody on board and on land. They'll keep women for their extracurricular activities. Are there any children on board?"

"Yes, teenagers."

"They'll keep them too. Teenage girls are highly sought after. The boys will be recruited, and it won't be like joining a sorority house. It will be brutal."

Lucas felt his phone vibrate. It was a text from June.

Ice buckets procured. In my cabin. All good.

He texted back. *Good. See you soon.*

They left the bridge separately. Tony going first, taking all but two of the guns Lucas had brought. He went off to form a posse.

Lucas stopped at the gift shop, checked on June, then headed to his cabin. Tosin joined him about twenty minutes later. They turned the TV on a little too loud and wrote notes to each other in the notebook that Lucas had just bought. They chatted for a bit and kept the conversation light; in case the room was bugged. Lucia's master card key was missing when they found her. They had to assume the gang had access to passenger cabins. They talked about June and George and Grace. Lucas told him about his love for the ocean. Tosin told him about the first time he saw the ocean in Tripoli.

"When I moved to Malta, I took a diving course," Tosin explained. "It allowed me to experience it on a grander scale, and I realized I could make money doing it. I came on this trip because I thought I was being hired for a job."

"Me too."

They didn't stay in their cabin long. Lucas hated being there at all, but constantly snooping around the ship would raise suspicion. He wanted to find every gang member on the ship and beat the crap out of them, but that would have to wait.

They met up with Tony to get an update. Since Tony had access to the whole ship, it was easier for him to find a place where they could talk. Tony introduced the two men he had with him. "This is Chuck, he's one of our engineers. He's great with electronics. Knows lots of stuff."

Chuck nodded hello.

"And this is Sam. He's an assistant in the medical center. He knows all about medications and how to knock somebody out with something other than blunt force trauma. I tried to start with people I think we may need the most. I've recruited others, including one who works in the galley and one who works in the dining room. Their instructions are to act normal and watch for anything suspicious."

"So, what's the plan?" Lucas asked. "Sulieman, can we get the weapons? I'd really like the gang to not have access to those."

"If we try to take them, try to move them or try to keep the gang from getting to them, we're in for a fight. Honestly, our best option is reaching the continent without them knowing we're onto them. Once the other ships arrive, we'll have backup and the element of surprise."

"That means we have to leave Suha where she is until then."

"Believe me, I know. I hate it. We need a plan for defending the ship and the passengers if it comes to a fight before we reach the continent and we need a plan for defeating the gang once we have back up. It is most likely that not only will there be ships on our side; there will be ships on their side as well."

"Then there's no way we're getting out of this without a fight. Even if we somehow manage to miraculously take out every gang member on this ship, there will still be at least one ship to deal with when we reach Antarctica."

"Correct. They've been working on this plan for months. We just found out about it two hours ago."

They talked about their options. Chuck and Sam filled them in on what skills and knowledge they had. They were both smart and capable – and not about to back down. Tony knew he had to bring more people into the plan. The crew needed to know what they were up against.

He gave Chuck and Sam the task of picking crew members that they trusted the most and creating teams. Each team would have a team leader. Tony wanted teams to protect the bridge, the engine room, the med center and any other critical function areas. The remaining teams were to identify everything at their disposal that could be used to defend the ship and its passengers. Then make a plan to execute.

"Right down to the last bag of flour," Tony said. "Go 'Home Alone' ape shit on these guys."

"Got it," Sam said. He and Chuck went off to build their teams.

Tony said, "I've got to go check in with the captain and act like a purser for a while. I'll catch up with you guys later."

Lucas and Tosin were walking down a hallway when Tosin heard a whisper. "Tosin!" Tosin froze. Only three people on this boat knew his real name. He turned in the direction of the voice, and saw Nadil's head peeking out from behind a corner.

Tosin couldn't believe it. He mouthed the word *Nadil*?

Lucas whispered, "A good guy? Please tell me that's a good guy."

"That's Suha's brother, Nadil." Then Saif's head joined Nadil's from around the corner. A big smile on his face, considering the circumstances. "That's his brother, Saif." Tosin walked down to meet them. "What are you doing here?"

"Long story. Is Suha on board?"

"We need to talk," Tosin said.

Lucas had already tried his master key card on the room they had exited with Tony. It worked. The four men went in.

Tosin started, "You came here for Suha? You knew she was here?"

"Yes," Nadil replied. "I knew something was up while I was at work. I overheard a few conversations about oil in Antarctica. I didn't hear enough to know exactly what was going on, but I knew it wasn't good. I knew they wanted the oil. I started researching Antarctica. I found the news story about the oil found in the Weddell Sea. I found out that Antarctica has no government. There's no one entity with the power to protect it. Then Suha never came home from work. I knew that the gangs had infiltrated the Central Bank and Libyan Oil. I put the pieces together. I knew this was the last ship going to the continent until spring. I knew Suha had to be on it. I contacted Saif and told him everything. I told him I was going to Ushuaia. He said he was coming too. All of the cabins were booked. We came anyway. Maybe we could get to her before they got her onto the ship. Then the ship's departure got delayed, cabins became available, and we were able to book passage. We've been careful, trying not to be seen. We move around the ship at night, looking for anything that can help us find her. We saw you praying, but your friend here and the other guy came in before we could approach you. I'm telling you Tosin, Allah is helping us. I know it. I've been praying too."

Tosin nodded. "By the way, I've been Sulieman since I left Tripoli. It needs to stay that way. Forget Tosin. Call me Sulieman."

"Sulieman," Nadil repeated with a warm smile.

Lucas spoke up. "What is so special about Sulieman? Suha gave you that doe-eyed smile when you said it to her too."

Nadil answered. "Suliman is our last name, our family name." He looked at Tosin when he said that last part. Nadil continued, "Tosin, Suha told me she saw you on the street one day. She asked me not to tell Mom and Dad. They would have been heartbroken all over again. I hated losing you. It was the worst day of my life. You're my best friend. I am so sorry."

"I know. It was my fault. You told me not to do it and I didn't listen," Tosin added, "I paid dearly for that. When I left Tripoli, I asked for Sulieman as a first name. It was easy to remember, and it reminded me of why I left everything I knew and loved for the second time in my life."

Lucas remembered what Suha had said about Tosin's three days in the back of a truck but now was not the time for that story.

"You've seen Suha? Where is she?" Saif asked.

"The gang has her," Tosin said. "She's safe for now."

"What do you mean the gang has her?" Saif was angry. "You've talked to her? Why does the gang have her? I came here for my sister. Let's go get her."

"It's not that simple," Tosin said. "We can't let the gang know we're onto them. Freeing Suha would start a war on this ship."

"I don't care. Then we'll fight. I'm done with the gangs controlling my life and threatening my family. This has to end."

"Even if by some miracle we win this battle, it won't stop the power and control that the gangs have in Tripoli."

Saif gave a head sweep, as if motioning to the rest of the world. "It would if anybody cared."

"Yeah," Lucas said. "We've had this discussion, about the rhinos."

"It won't end with the rhinos."

"I know. It's not right. It's not fair."

"Fair?" Saif hissed. "It's wrong. On so many levels."

Silence. He wasn't wrong.

Finally, Lucas spoke. "We've got to stop the gang and their whole plan. They cannot take control of any part of Antarctica. We need all the help we can get. Are you guys in?"

"I don't know why we should be. I say we just get our sister and take care of ourselves. No one cares about Libya. Why should we care about a big block of ice?"

"Because we can't let them control anything else, Saif, and you know it. You just said it yourself: this has to end." Nadil continued, "They'll destroy Antarctica to get what they want. Antarctica is bigger than the United States. It's bigger than all of Europe. What do you think is going to happen if massive ice sheets bigger than Texas start breaking off and melting in warmer ocean waters? The repercussions will be global. Once something like that happens, it can't be undone. The planet will lose a lot more than rhinos. Sea levels will rise. Tripoli could end up under water. Are you willing to let that happen?"

"If we survive this, we're leaving Tripoli anyway. All of us. I'm not giving Mom and Dad a choice." Saif closed his eyes and sighed, coming to a decision. "I'm in."

"Me too," Nadil added.

Chapter 12:

The Plan

Tosin turned to Lucas, "Now that we have these two on the team, freeing Suha needs to be top priority. We will reach the continent tomorrow. Whatever we're going to do, we need to do it tonight. If they plan on taking the ship, they will most likely put everything they need in place overnight and try to take the ship tomorrow. We need to get Suha out of there. Tomorrow will be too late."

"Agreed."

"Where is she?" Saif asked.

"I'm not telling you," Tosin replied. "I won't have you rushing to her rescue and getting both of you killed."

"We've left the weapons in place so they don't know we're onto them," Lucas said. "I think we need to move them, so they'll be at our disposal, not theirs. We need to find Tony. It's time to act."

They left the room separately. They decided they each needed to do something that seemed normal before meeting up with Tony. Nadil and Saif would do their best not be seen. They knew they would be recognized by the gang members immediately. Lucas sent Tony a text asking if he could get more fish from the lower deck for George and Grace, then he would go check on June. Tosin would pray.

Before they went their separate ways, Lucas said, "We'll meet where the fish is kept on the lower deck in thirty minutes and try to move the weapons. Empty your luggage and bring it with you."

Lucas stopped at his cabin first. He emptied his rolling luggage and smashed one of the wheels. He put his empty backpack and the bags he had put the weapons in that he had brought up previously. Then he went to June's cabin and filled her in on everything that had happened since he last saw her.

"I just can't believe it," June said. "What are the odds? That Sulieman's, I mean Tosin's, adopted siblings are here on the ship?" She paused. "Do you trust them? All of them?"

"I have to. We don't have a choice at this point."

"Nadil is right. Protecting Antarctica is protecting the entire planet. Lucas, you can bring Suha here if you need to. Please save her. I don't want anybody to die on this ship, including you. Well, maybe the gang."

"That's the plan. Hey, can I have your luggage? It's for a good cause."

"Take it. Go forth and conquer."

Lucas handed her the master card key that Tony had given him. "This will get you into lots of places on the ship, including cabins. If you need to get out of here, take George and Grace and hide."

George and Grace had insisted on being let out of the cage when Lucas walked in. Now they were happily waddling about the cabin, pooping as they went. "I might have to vacate just because of the smell," June said. "Oh, and Lucas – Grace is pregnant."

"Great, I think."

"I know."

Lucas left to meet Tony and the others, dragging two pieces of roller luggage with him. His suitcase with the broken wheel, and June's smeared with penguin poop. "I gotta try to get these fixed up so they're usable. I can't do it in my cabin." This excuse seemed to satisfy the onlookers with their confused expressions.

When he arrived, everyone else was there. Otherwise, the area seemed empty. "I've got more people coming," Tony said. "I told Sam and Chuck to come down with the team leaders. We all need to know what the plan is."

"Ok," Lucas said. "I thought we could fill the suitcases with the weapons and send them up in the service elevator."

"I figured that was your plan," Tony said. "We've got people standing by to keep prying eyes away from that area for a while."

They started loading up the suitcases. Chuck and Sam and several team leaders joined them a few minutes later. "How do we protect the passengers?" Chuck asked. "Do we come up with an excuse and have the captain make an announcement to keep them all in their cabins?"

Tosin spoke up. "Two reasons I think that's a no. A: We're pretty sure the gang has access to at least one master key card, probably more than one. B: Short of the captain announcing that a gang is trying to take over the ship and will kill any passengers that leave their cabins, people are going to leave their cabins. We'll be nearing Antarctica. This is what they paid to come see. Plus, they need to eat."

"Are we going to risk letting them eat in the dining room? What if we had the cabin stewards deliver food and beverages to the cabins?" Sam asked. "You know, Sorry for the trouble folks. Thank you for your patience and understanding. Here's some food and beverages for you to enjoy." Then he added, "Just don't eat it until tomorrow, when the shit hits the fan."

Lucas answered, "I like that idea, but it might raise suspicion. We only know of one cabin occupied by the gang. There must be more."

Tony spoke, "We've got people handling the food as best they can. Identifying everything that should be safe for consumption and stashing it away. Pretty sure we've identified who was put in place to taint the food. We'll take them out if we have to. Bottom line, we believe they're making their move in the morning, and we can't serve breakfast in the dining room. Delivering food to the cabins may be our best option. The captain may have to make that announcement. I'm not sure there's any other way."

They finished loading the suitcases and sent them up the elevator. The gang couldn't possibly know that their plan had been discovered. Otherwise, they would have been guarding the weapons much more closely. It seemed that they were intentionally staying away from them until they were needed to avoid suspicion. They left the crates in place. No one would know the weapons were gone until the crates were opened.

"This is another blessing from Allah.", Nadil said. "It is a miracle we were able to get these weapons out of here without getting caught."

Lucas sent June a text. *Mission accomplished.* She would know what that meant.

Tosin's mind had been swirling with thoughts and questions the entire time they were loading the suitcases. He didn't know how many gang members were on board. He couldn't identify all of them. He didn't know what their plan was. He couldn't be sure he could make the right decisions. Ones that would keep his friends and the passengers alive. It frustrated him. "If only I knew what their plan was," he said aloud in his frustration.

"I can help with that."

Tosin froze. He knew that voice. He closed his eyes, silently praying it wasn't true. He wasn't here. He couldn't be. That voice haunted his nightmares. So many times, he had woken up screaming in a cold sweat, expecting to see him standing there.

He opened his eyes and looked at the men he considered his friends. They were slowly readying the pistols that they had kept from the crates. Tosin turned to face the voice.

"Hey Tosin. You have something that belongs to me. I want it back."

Blade.

Shit.

Chapter 13:

Penguins Unite

Blade was leaning against the wall on one shoulder, like he was the coolest cat in the world. He seemed very confident. That made Tosin very nervous. Tosin knew why he was here and exactly what he wanted.

"I don't have anything of yours," Tosin lied.

"Listen Tosin, do you think you're here for a diving job? Do you think snatching Suha was their idea?" Blade took a few steps forward. "They had completely forgotten that you even existed, but I didn't. I've searched your place in Malta, it wasn't there. I've searched your cabin. Not there either. You'd better have it on you."

Tosin heard Nadil behind him mutter under his breath, "Tosin, what have you done?"

He saw the tattoo on Blade's arm, just past his wrist. "You joined them."

"Had to. I needed them to get to you."

Tosin saw the look on Blade's face when he spoke those words. Blade wasn't the same person he had left in Tripoli. It was apparent that he had experienced horrors that no human being should ever have to endure. Tosin took a few steps back. He felt Lucas gently grab his arm and pull him back, into the group. A show of solidarity. *We have guns. Looks like you don't.*

Blade stood still, assessing the situation. Lucas felt his phone vibrate.

"You said you could help us," Lucas said. "Why would you help us?"

"I just want what's rightfully mine. I don't give a rat's ass about that place." Blade gave a head sweep, motioning to the world outside of the ship. "I went to a lot of trouble to get to you Tosin. I told you to never cross me. I want it back."

"Tosin, what is he talking about?" Saif asked.

"I don't know." Tosin had so many responses swirling around in his head. So many retorts and accusations that he wanted to hurl at Blade. He hated him for everything he had put him through. That day he ran into Suha was one of the best things that had ever happened to him. It forced him to see the truth through Blade's lies. It forced him to leave Tripoli. Yeah, he took something when he left. Blade deserved it. Blade didn't appreciate anything, or anyone. The time he spent in Malta was the calmest and most serene time he had ever had in his life. It was magical. It allowed him to focus, re-evaluate his life and become a human being again. Now here they were. He had taken something that didn't belong to him and the consequence, once again, was Blade.

"How long have you been down here?" Tony asked.

"Long enough to know what happened to the weapons." Blade spoke slowly, as if enjoying every moment. "Maybe I tipped the gang off to what you were doing. Maybe they intercepted the weapons and are on the decks above us, killing everyone as we speak. Maybe your precious penguins are already dead. I hear they're better than wood for making a fire. They burn great."

Tosin heard Lucas's breath quicken. Lucas was seething, which is exactly what Blade wanted. "Don't listen to him," Tosin said. "He's a master manipulator. What he just said is exactly what he didn't do." The look on Blade's face told Tosin he was right.

Blade spoke, "I have something you need. You have something I want. It's that simple."

Tony was agitated. "People are not going to die over your stupid little spat. What exactly is it that you're willing to kill for?"

"A dagger. A Tebu Arm Knife. Been in my family for generations."

"So," Tony said slowly with a patronizing tone, "you're willing to kill everyone on board over a dagger?" Blade's eyes hardened. Tosin cringed. Blind rage was not something you wanted to bring out of Blade.

"I killed everyone in my own gang over this dagger. It was part of my initiation. So, yeah."

Tosin closed his eyes. His stomach lurched. Dragon, Lefty, Pyro and Mac. Gone. Betrayed by the one person they should have been able to trust. He knew Blade wouldn't stop until he had the dagger, or he was dead.

"I say we just shoot him," said one of the team leads.

"Tosin, I know you better than anyone here," Nadil said. "Where's the dagger?"

"I don't have it. Besides, even if I gave it to him right now, do you think we can trust him?"

Silence. Blade had to be stopped. There was no other way.

BANG! A gunshot. All the men hit the floor, looking at each other, trying to figure out who had fired. Every one of them was just as surprised and confused as the next. Blade crumpled to the floor, screaming in pain. Blood oozing from his leg. Behind him stood Suha and June. They each had a pistol in their hand. Suha's was still raised in the air.

"I can't believe I hit him. I just wanted to distract him," Suha said. "Son of a bitch. He had it coming. I hate him." Then she looked at the group. "Nadil? Saif? You're here?" She ran to them and hugged her brothers. "I am so happy to see you. You came for me? How did you know? Are Mom and Dad okay?"

"Long story," Saif answered. "I put Mom and Dad in hiding."

"Suha, did you know Blade?" Tony asked.

"He's the one that snatched me from work and smacked me around. Piece of shit."

Lucas walked over to June. June started, "I know you're going to tell me we shouldn't have come down here, but...". Lucas just pulled her close and kissed her lips. All he wanted at that moment was to hold her. June was startled, but it didn't take long for her to return his kiss.

When their lips parted, he smiled. "You got some 'splainin to do."

"Yeah, I know," she said. They walked back over to the group. By now a few of the team leaders had surrounded Blade.

"How did you get free?" Nadil asked Suha.

Suha motioned to June. "June came to my rescue."

June explained, "I used the key card you gave me to get into the cabin. I stood outside of the door, listening for voices. All I heard was snoring."

"Moose," Suha said.

"Apparently he sleeps a lot," June said. "I opened the door slowly and sure enough, Moose was out. I knocked him out with a lamp and untied Suha. We tied him up and gagged him. Took his gun and key card too. This was all after I got your mission accomplished text. I went to the dining area to confirm that the weapons were safe. I even convinced them to give me a gun. I simply told them we were in for a fight, and I was not going to die because I was unarmed. I also may have thrown in the fact that I need to protect George and Grace for good measure. No decent human being wants them dead. I didn't even have to bring up the fact that Grace is pregnant, but I was ready to play that card if I had to."

"Grace is pregnant?" Tony exclaimed.

June nodded, smiling like a proud Grandma. "She's carrying an egg."

June continued, "I know that this puts an end to 'business as usual'. The jig is up. They know we're onto them. Lucas, I knew you were right when you said we have to free Suha tonight. We're down to the last few hours. We'll be there tomorrow. I had to get her out of there. I just knew I had to."

Tony sent a text from his phone. Everyone's phone vibrated. They looked at him for an explanation. "I made a group text of everyone that is in on the plan.

Everyone that has been preparing for battle. We knew at some point that things would start to unravel. Eventually we would have to defend this ship and everyone on it. Well, the good guys, I mean. Some of us decided on a phrase that would indicate when that moment came. So, they knew to be on high alert. I just sent it."

"What's the phrase?"

"Penguins unite."

"Suha, how often was anyone besides Moose with you in the room?" Lucas asked.

"When we left Ushuaia, there were people in there all the time. I think they were trying to lay low. Then they started getting bored and complaining about being cooped up and not being able to enjoy the cruise. Little by little they left. Moose was the only one in the room since this morning. Except when you found me."

"That could buy us some time. If no one checks the room, they won't know Suha is missing. If no one comes down here, they won't know the weapons are missing – and if no one goes looking for this guy, they won't know he's missing."

"It's Blade; and you'll never get away with it. You're all going to die."

"If I die, I'm taking you with me," Lucas said.

"If I find your dagger, I'll make sure you get buried with it," Tosin sneered. He saw a hint of sadness in Blade's eyes.

"If you find my dagger and I'm dead, return it to my father."

"What's his name?"

"Salhana. Salhana Ammar."

Sam spoke up, "Blade, why did you let us take the weapons?"

"I told you, I don't care about their stupid land dispute. I don't care about the oil. I don't want to have to pick up a gun tomorrow and start shooting people. Oh sure, they promised me riches, but that's never gonna happen. I'm not stupid. I'm using them. They're using me. When they're done with me, they'll kill me."

"And you think we won't?"

"You're the good guys. Good guys with comfy lives and a soft warm bed to sleep in every night don't kill people."

"We do if we have to."

"Then I won't give you a reason to have to. Patch up my leg, tie me up. Hide me somewhere and I'll be happy to wait for the carnage to end."

Sam stepped forward, demanding Blade's attention. "We know the Russians are in on it; and they've got ships there waiting for us." A flash of panic in Blaze's eyes. Tosin's hunch was right.

Lucas heard Tony on his phone. He had just sent a message.

Sam continued, "We know that all ship communications are being monitored, including all cell phones."

Blade gave the slightest eye roll. Not true. Good.

"We know that most of the gang members have never been on a ship before; and many of them are seasick."

A hint of respect in Blade's eyes that said, you guys are actually pretty good. True.

"We know that the gang has master key cards and plan on entering the cabins and killing the passengers and crew."

A flash of confusion in Blade's eyes. Not true.

"Actually, we know they plan to poison the food. Thanks."

"For what?"

"For helping us out."

"I haven't told you anything."

"Yes, you have."

Tony spoke up, "We need to get out of here. We've got a crew up above in charge of defending this ship and we have no idea what's going on up there."

Lucas motioned to Blade. "We can't leave him here. They'll be coming down for the weapons at some point."

"Right. Let's gag him and find someplace to stash him. Make sure he's tied up real tight."

As they had been doing all day, they left separately to avoid suspicion. Nidal and Saif took Suha with them. "We've gotten pretty good at not being seen," Saif said. The team leads left to get back to their teams. Tony went to talk to the captain. Lucas and June went to check on the birds.

Back at June's cabin, June let the birds out of the cage and tended to them. Lucas could see the sadness and pain on her face. She was scared. Scared that George and Grace might never step foot on their homeland again. That they might not get the chance to raise their baby.

"Lucas, if it comes to it," she said with tears in her eyes, "please save them. Whatever it takes. Save them first. Make sure they get home."

Lucas felt himself choking up. He fought back the tears he could feel forming behind his eyes. "Don't talk like that. Don't say goodbye. We both have more living to do. George and Grace too. We'll get through this. I promise." He pulled her close and held her. George and Grace watched them, then cuddled up against their legs. They knew something was wrong.

Tony had checked in with the captain and was making the rounds, checking on the teams. Everything on the ship seemed normal. The gang had not yet made their move. He was going to spend every second trying to make sure they had every advantage he could think of. He had already checked on several areas, including the engine room and the med center.

At the med center, he checked on Anna. She was still there. Conscious and resting. Jakob was there too. He was polite and cordial. He didn't act anything like the man who had boarded the ship the day before. The dynamics of their relationship seemed to have changed. It seemed Anna was the alpha now. While he was there, he talked to Sam too. "That was impressive, what you did down below. You interrogated Blade without interrogating him."

"Yeah. I focused on reading people during my med training. People lie to doctors all the time. Victims of domestic abuse lie, drug addicts lie, kids who get hurt doing things they knew they weren't supposed to do lie. Reading faces comes in handy. You can learn a lot from someone's eyes if you pay attention."

Now Tony was at the dining room, talking with the head chef, Sasha. The plan to poison the food really bothered him. He needed to be sure that everything possible was being done to protect the passengers. "Do you think you have enough food available that can't be tainted?"

"Yes. I've changed the dinner menu. I realize that might look suspicious, but it's the best way to ensure we control the food. The menus are planned way in advance. They would have known what was going to be served. That's what they would have poisoned, so I changed it. We've kept everybody we don't trust out of here."

"How?"

"I have my ways. Speaking of that, the teams have done a pretty good job of identifying who is playing for the opposing team. We can use their own plan against them. I can make them real sick. They still need to eat, and I got the food."

"Do it. Just don't make the passengers sick."

"I can manage that. You know, if we delivered food to the cabins and the passengers got sick, they would all stay in their cabins. Not too sick. Just sick enough."

Tony sighed. "You're not wrong, but I'm not willing to do that yet. The passengers are our first priority."

"Keeping them alive is our first priority. Not wining and dining them. Not anymore. At some point you're going to need to ask yourself; do the passengers deserve to know? Should they be able to choose whether they fight for their own survival or hide in their cabin?"

Tony didn't say anything. She was right. "It may not come to that. If it does, I'll let the captain make that decision."

He sent Lucas a text. *Where are you?*

The reply came back, June's 312.

He headed to June's cabin to give them an update. When Lucas opened the door, the smell was intense. "Oh man, that is awful!" He peered around Lucas into the cabin. Bird poop everywhere. "I am so getting fired for this."

"You get used to it after a while. But yeah, it's pretty bad."

Tony told them what he had learned from visiting the teams. He added, "I wonder if they know their weapons are gone. Our teams are armed. Any extra weapons were locked up."

"Good to know. Thanks. Do you need me for anything?"

"No. Just lay low for a while. I don't think any of us are sleeping tonight. I'll let you know of the first sign of trouble."

The dinner hour came and went with no casualties. The bulk of the drama came from passengers complaining about the lackluster meal. They expected better. The dining room attendants told the passengers that, due to unforeseen circumstances, the dinner that had been planned for the evening had to be changed. They weren't lying. Tony tried not to hover around the dining room like a mother hen, but he couldn't help it. In his mind, he kept seeing passengers dying. Collapsing on the floor in a crumpled heap and faces landing in a plate full of food.

As the passengers finished their meals and the dining room cleared out, Sasha came and stood next to Tony. "See? I told you I had it under control."

"Great job. The dining room didn't seem nearly as full as it was last night."

"That's because most of the opposing team is so sick they can barely stand up. They'll recover, but not until after we reach Antarctica. If they contact the med center for relief, Sam and the others will make sure they stay sick."

Tony was so relieved that he was visibly shaking. We might just get through this. "Thank you, Sasha. You are amazing. This crew is amazing. I am so hungry. I've barely eaten all day. Do you have enough left for one more?"

"Absolutely."

The crew slept in shifts that night, at least two people awake on each team at all times. Most of them did not return to their cabins. They knew the gang had to know they were onto them. They hoped they were too sick to do anything about it.

Lucas stayed with June. Tony had sent a message that it looked like most of the gang members were too sick to leave their cabins. They were hoping to get through the night with no uprisings. He stayed in touch with Tony and Tosin to make sure things were still copasetic. The smell in June's cabin was no longer bearable. Since Lucas's cabin was down the hall, they relocated to his cabin. "We don't have to put them in the cage to move them. I have modified harnesses for them; and leashes."

"You need diapers for them too."

"Well, I never thought they would end up staying in my room."

They got settled in Lucas's cabin. "Mi casa es su casa," Lucas smiled.

"Do you speak Spanish?" June asked. "I always thought your accent sounded kind of French. It's a beautiful accent, by the way."

"I speak Dutch, which is the official language of Suriname. It is English based, but if I wrote you a letter in Dutch, you wouldn't be able to read it. Since English is spoken pretty much everywhere, and it's hard to travel outside of your own country and not speak it – I learned that too."

The time together gave Lucas a chance to learn more about her. "I've been wondering, did you bring George and Grace from New York?"

"No. I brought them from Buenos Aires. I've been working at a wildlife sanctuary. They rehabilitate penguins there."

"How did you end up there?"

"I attended a bird fair in South America. I didn't want to just work at the zoo in New York, or spend the rest of my life studying pigeons. I wanted to spread my wings. Pun intended." June continued, "I met some wonderful people at the bird fair. One meeting led to another and I was asked to work there. I didn't go to the fair to find a job. I hadn't even considered working outside of the United States until then. I received a few offers, which I was not expecting at all. I chose that one. I didn't choose it because of the penguins specifically. I just really liked how they seemed to treat and care for their animals."

They had stretched out on the bed, clothes on. It was the most comfortable place in the room. "Do you still live in Suriname?"

"No. I live in Barra Mansa now. It's between Rio and Sao Paulo. I lived in Rio for a while. I got to the point where I needed to get out of the city. Barra

Mansa is a nice place. Much quieter. Plus, it's easy to travel to Rio or Sao Paulo if I need to. They have a zoo there. I've never been to it. I think it's a small one."

"Mmm," June murmured. Her head was resting on his shoulder. He could tell she was close to drifting off to sleep. "Go ahead and sleep. I'm not tired. Will George and Grace sleep all night?"

"Penguins don't sleep for hours at a time. They sleep for seconds at a time. All day and all night. They'll be up to keep you company."

"Great." June couldn't tell if his response was sincere or sarcastic.

Lucas turned on the TV and put it on mute so June could sleep. He wanted to be able to hear everything going on outside of his room. He didn't really care what they were saying on the TV anyway. He just needed something to look at. George and Grace calmed down and went into their cage. They didn't sleep much. Occasionally they would waddle out, stretch their legs and toddle up to the edge of the bed to be petted.

Lucas didn't sleep much. He knew that because of how many times he had looked at the clock. 11:32 pm, 12:06 am, 1:21 am, 2:15am, 3:09am, 4:41am.

At 5:55 am, he got a text from Tony. *Are you up?*

He replied, *Yeah, been up all night. Couldn't sleep.*

A message came back, *Me either. I'm on my way to you.*

He hated disturbing June, but he needed to move. He had laid still most of the night and his arm was asleep. He slowly got up and went to splash some water on his face. A few minutes later, there was a light tap on the door. Lucas looked through the peephole. Tony. He opened the door. Tony had come bearing gifts. Coffee!

"Thanks. I really need this. You're a lifesaver."

"You're welcome. I brought a couple of energy drinks, too. The sun will be up soon."

They both stood there, replaying the events that had brought them to this moment. "You know," Tony said, "Lucia was found less than 24 hours ago. So much has happened since then. She's the one that saved us. If she hadn't walked into that cabin, if we hadn't found her, we may have never known what was going on right under our noses."

"We need to honor her."

"Oh, we will."

By now June was up, standing next to them. George and Grace were leaning against her legs like a couple of clingy two-year-olds.

Lucas handed her a coffee. "Thank you so much.", she said, lowering her nose to the cup and taking a deep breath. "I'm going to see if these two will eat. I'm guessing it's going to be a long day, no matter what happens."

"June, Tony and I are going to go out and see what's going on. Please stay here. The sun will be up soon."

"Okay, but I really want to see Antarctica."

"Oh, you will.", Tony said. "As soon as we take out the trash."

Lucas and Tony headed to the ship's bow. They knew they were near the continent, and they wanted to know what lay ahead of them. Through the window in the pre-dawn darkness was a scene they never would have imagined. It instilled sheer terror in both of them.

Ahead of them, four ships, side by side, blocking their path.

Hovering in front of those ships, four helicopters.

Shit.

Chapter 14:

Taking Out The Trash

Tony grabbed his radio. "Captain?"

"I see them Tony. They're on our side."

The calvary is here. It's over.

Lucas motioned his head toward the deck, "Can we?"

"I think so." They stepped out on deck.

The four helicopters flew forward and people began to repel onto the deck from the one directly over the bow.

The first man onto the deck introduced himself. "Mr. Matera?" he asked, extending his hand. "Sergeant Rugger, U.S. Army. Pleased to meet you, sir."

Tony shook his hand and stared in disbelief as one by one, the helicopters took turns hovering over the deck. Men and women repelled onto the deck from each one. They wore different uniforms. They were not all U.S. Army; and they were not all military. Tony motioned to Lucas. "This is Mr. Kalloe."

"Mr. Kalloe, pleased to meet you. Are you the passenger that's been helping the crew get through this?"

"Not the only one. We've had help."

Tony watched as the men and women landing on the deck immediately infiltrated the ship. "They have their orders?"

"Yes. They know who they're going after. Getting the intel from the captain yesterday gave us time to do some recon, while at the same time planning a rescue. Everyone agreed that this was most likely an attempt at a land grab of the Antarctic Peninsula. Truth is, most governments expected this to happen. They just didn't expect it so soon. Two Libyan vessels were captured. They were heavily armed. Way too many weapons for research vessels. They put up a good fight. It was only because we had choppers at our disposal that we were able to overtake them."

"I can't believe you pulled this off so quickly."

"Me neither. Thirteen countries with research bases on or near the Antarctic Peninsula agreed to help. Once they knew what was happening, every single one of them was given permission to join the mission. They all had a ship in the area getting ready to return to the mainland for the winter. Initially, there was some bickering and squabbling over who should do what and who got to be in charge and blah, blah, blah. The President of the United States ordered mobilization of troops in USSOUTHCOM. He said he'd send U.S. troops no matter what, while the other countries wasted time bickering. That got their attention. They didn't want the U.S. to get sole credit for the rescue. They quickly became a lot more cooperative. I tell ya; the President is not a man to be trifled with."

"So I've heard."

Members of the rescue team began returning, escorting their prisoners, most of whom looked too sick to care. One prisoner was speaking in Arabic.

"Anybody know what he's saying?" Sergeant Rugger asked.

"He said he wants to see a doctor. He's been sick all night. Don't blame him if he shits his pants on the chopper. They all seem to be very sick, sir."

Sergeant Rugger looked at Tony, questioning. "Compliments of our head chef," Tony explained.

Sergeant Rugger smiled. "Brilliant. Makes my job easier."

Lucas spoke up. "Thirteen countries, you said?"

"Yeah, you see these four ships? There are four more standing by behind these. A second line of defense if needed. It took four ships to overtake the Libyans, and there's one anchored at the continent."

"Impressive.", Lucas said.

"Yeah, I wouldn't have believed it if I hadn't been a part of it. They all set aside their differences for the greater good; and all within hours. One of the bases on the peninsula is Ukrainian. You know they aren't going to let the Russians move in if they have any say in it. Antarctica is just too important. It cannot become a war zone. It cannot become a killing zone. We can't allow it to be exploited. The repercussions would be global, and probably fatal to mankind. Most people go about their lives barely conscious of the fact that it even exists or that their lives depend on protecting it."

"What's the plan for the passengers?" Tony asked.

"Evacuate them. Today. The cruise line does not want the ship to make the return trip with passengers on board. They feel it's too risky. The research vessels can get everybody back to the mainland; but they can't provide the vacation that these people came for. Unfortunately, the vacation that never really got started ends today."

The sun had risen but it was cloudy. The wind was picking up. Passengers started coming out onto the deck, wanting answers. Tosin was one of them. With the rescue team on board, crew members that had remained at their posts to protect the ship now had approval to leave their posts and tend to the alarmed passengers.

Tony grabbed his radio. "Captain, what do you want me to tell these people?"

The answer came back. "Any passengers that want to leave the ship now may do so, if the rescue team can accommodate them. All passengers must evacuate today, no exceptions. I will personally address everyone that remains on the ship this morning. Sasha gave me an idea. We're going to do it. I'll fill you in later."

Tony smiled. *Sasha is in on this? Oh, this should be good.*

Lucas heard a familiar "Honk!" behind him. He even knew the owner of that particular honk. That was Grace. He turned to see June practically being dragged by two very excited penguins. "I figured it was safe to come out now and these guys needed a walk."

"I've heard about these two as well," the sergeant said, motioning to the penguins.

"I need to take them to El Polo Sur."

"We'll get them there."

"I'm going with them."

"Ma'am, my orders are to evacuate all passengers. As far as I know, you're a passenger. I have no orders that allow you to continue to the base."

"I need to talk to someone in charge at El Polo Sur. They're expecting the penguins; and they're expecting me to deliver them. That's what I'm going to do."

"I'll see what I can do, ma'am."

"Sergeant," Tony said, "if you have everything under control out here, I'd like to go inside for a bit."

"Absolutely. I don't think there's anyone left on this ship to give you any trouble."

With the ship pitching back and forth, they walked mid-ship to head back inside. The waves were spraying onto the deck, making the trek even more difficult. Tosin joined them. Then they saw something at the ship's stern that made them freeze in their tracks.

"I want my dagger."

Blade. And he had a hostage. Jakob Haas, with a knife positioned at his torso.

"He's got my kids," Jakob said. Lucas's heart sank. The teenagers on board were Jakob and Anna's.

"We can't call for help. He'll kill him."

"Exactly," Blade hissed. "Well, Tosin? Your move."

"Fine. You win. I've got your knife. You can have it."

"Good. Tell you what. You walk to me so we can go get it. When you do, I'll release pretty boy here."

"I'm not going anywhere without my kids."

"You can have your spoiled little brats back once I get what I came for."

"No deal. I'm going to be on you like flies on shit until I've got my kids."

"Jakob," Lucas started, "maybe it's best if you come with us. We'll get your kids back. I promise." Jakob's eyes hardened. Lucas could see the rage building. He was glad this time that rage wasn't directed at him.

"What's going on here?" came a voice from behind them. It was Sam.

"Blade took his kids. Still wants the knife."

"Get lost," Blade hissed. "or I'll hurt him real bad."

Sam studied Blade for a few seconds. "No, you won't. He's your bargaining chip. You need him to get what you want."

"I need him alive, that's all. Severely damaged is fine with me."

George and Grace had been getting increasingly agitated. June knelt down slowly, watching Blade the whole time. "I just need to calm them a bit, that's all."

"Don't try anything."

"Oh, I won't. You're the boss. You're in charge here." She petted the birds and spoke in soothing tones.

"So, you took his kids? Did you take their cell phones?" Sam asked.

Blade's attention turned to Sam, then his eyes shot down, thinking. They're tied up. Why would I take those? I don't care about their stupid phones. All he wanted was the dagger.

The ship pitched backward, as it crested a wave, and all Blade saw was two penguins headed straight at him, sliding on their bellies like a couple of torpedoes. June came sliding down right behind them, on her left butt cheek, right leg extended straight out. On contact, Blade and Jakob fell like bowling pins. The knife flew out of Blade's hand. George and Grace wasted no time pecking at Blade, seemingly berating him with their angry squawks. Lucas had followed her cue and slid down as well. He wanted to get to them as soon as possible, and that was the fastest way. June quickly started to try to wrap the leashes around Blade's wrists. Jakob had slid off to the side and was having trouble getting his footing. The ship pitched forward. Blade was thrashing and kicking, trying to get away. They stood him up. He kept his weight on one leg.

He was obviously in pain. Jakob got to his feet and was now trying to help subdue Blade. June still didn't have him secured with the leashes. The struggle was more than Blade's injured leg could take. He was trying to maintain his foothold with one good leg. Tosin, Tony and Sam arrived; all trying to help. The ship pitched back again. Blade had six people trying to subdue him, their weight now pressing on him as the ship pitched. With no solid foothold, he went backwards over the railing.

"No!" June screamed. She still had hold of the wet leashes. Blade's weight shift instantly pulled her to the railing. Lucas got behind her and used his weight to anchor her. He grabbed the leashes and held on with her. Tosin leaned over the railing. Blade was dangling from the back of the ship, hanging onto the leashes. They were partially wrapped around his wrists, but he was slipping. Tosin reached out to him. "C'mon Blade, grab my hand."

"We both know I'm not going to make it. I can't hold on with one hand. These things are way too slippery. Letting go has only one outcome for me."

"We can pull you up. Just hold on."

"For what? To go to jail? They'll send me back to Tripoli. The gangs have infiltrated everything there. They have people everywhere. I won't last two days. Not even in police custody. I played a big part in orchestrating this plan. Its failure will be blamed on me. My death will be brutal. I told you I knew they would kill me when they were done with me. I had a plan. A way out. Now I guess this is my way out. I can never go back. It's okay. I think it's for the best. Promise me you'll return the dagger to my father. It's all I really want. I should have never taken it from him in the first place."

"I will. I promise. Salhana Ammar. I haven't forgotten."

Blade smiled, let go and disappeared into the Southern Ocean. Tosin watched, looking to see if he surfaced. Nothing. He turned back to the group. "It was his choice."

"How am I gonna find my kids? We don't know where he put them?" Jakob asked.

"Do you have your cell phone?" Sam asked.

"That asshole threw it overboard."

"How about Anna's phone?"

"It's in our cabin."

"Please tell me you have some type of family location tracking on your phones."

"Well yeah, we've got teenagers."

"Good. I don't think Blade took their phones. We just need Anna's phone to track them. I'll go with you to make sure the kids are okay and haven't been harmed."

"Thanks Sam," Tony said. "I'm going up to the bow to check in with the sergeant."

"I'll go with you," Lucas said. Sam and Jakob went to find the kids while the rest of the group made their way back to the bow.

At the bow, Tony checked in with Rugger. "How's it going?"

"Amazingly well. Your team did a fantastic job of setting this rescue up for success. This could have been so much worse."

"Thanks. This ship does have an amazing crew. How did you know exactly who to go after when you boarded the ship?"

"The initial recon revealed a group of cabins that were all booked together, using the same credit card. Room 204 was one of them. The credit card belonged to a shell company, but it didn't take much to track the card to the Libyan bank and the organized crime that's a part of it. Once we had that information, it wasn't too hard to figure out which crew members were part of the gang."

Tony nodded. "Do you have any passengers that want to evacuate immediately?"

"No. All of the passengers that I've spoken to had no idea their lives were in danger until this morning. This mission has gone so smoothly, most of them are not too concerned. They feel safe. Everyone that I've spoken to wants to hear what the captain has to say. They know they have to evacuate today anyway."

A member of the rescue team walked up. "Looks like we've got everybody except Jalal Ammar."

Tony turned to Lucas. "Jalal must be Blade's real name."

"Who is Blade?" the sergeant asked.

"Jalal Ammar, we knew him as Blade. He just went overboard at the stern. He had a hostage. It couldn't be helped," Tosin said.

"Somebody went overboard? He had a hostage? Is the hostage okay? I really need to know these things." The sergeant was more than a little perturbed. He spoke into his radio. "Team, I have a report of Jalal Ammar going overboard off the stern. Can I get a chopper over there?"

"On our way," came the reply.

"The hostage, Jakob Haas is fine," Tony said. "Blade, Jalal, took his kids hostage first. Jakob and our crew member, Sam, went to find them."

Rugger rolled his eyes in frustration and grabbed his radio. "Got a report of two kids taken hostage. Anybody find them?"

"I'm with them, sir," came a voice over the radio. "Ran into their dad and a crew member looking for them. Tracked them via cell phone. They were right where the phone said they would be. They're both fine. Scared shitless, but fine."

The group breathed a collaborative sigh of relief.

June had been standing with the group; along with George and Grace. The birds had been fairly well-behaved, watching all of the commotion on the deck. They seemed to be trying to figure out the big noisy 'bird' on the deck. Occasionally there was a honk of disdain because no one was petting them.

Rugger looked at June. "May I?"

"Oh yes, of course. They love being the center of attention."

Rugger stroked their heads. "They're pretty cool," he said.

Tosin petted them too. "I've been wanting to meet them."

"You should've seen them do a belly slide a few minutes ago."

"Oh, I recorded it," offered a nearby passenger. It was one of the ladies they had sat with at dinner the first night on the ship. She walked toward the group and played the video on her phone. The video showed George, Grace, June and Lucas all sliding down the deck. Blade and Jakob were standing at the stern of the ship. From the angle of the recording, you couldn't see the knife ready to pierce Jakob's abdomen. The video ended when Blade and Jakob crumpled onto the deck. To the rest of the world, who had no idea that their lives were in danger, the video would be hysterical. "The ship was rocking, so that's all I got. I almost fell over recording that. Already uploaded it to social media, too. I can't believe it uploaded, but it did. People are going to love this. May I pet them?"

"Sure," June said. June wasn't sure how she felt about the video being out there for the world to see, but it was already done.

George and Grace quickly became the center of attention as everyone on the deck approached, asking to pet them.

After a few minutes, June announced to the group that had gathered, "I'm going to take them in now. They've had a busy morning. Plus, I'm wet and cold and hungry."

Tony smiled broadly. "I'm happy to announce that breakfast is available in the dining room, which is where the captain will be addressing everyone."

The ship had already sailed through the first blockade of four ships. The helicopters had taken turns landing on the deck to load up the prisoners. Now everyone on deck stood silently as the ship sailed through the next line of four ships. Crew members from all ships stood on deck cheering and clapping. Ships horns were blaring in celebration. It was a good day. They had saved an entire continent; at least for the time being.

"Looks like everyone that we came for is accounted for," Rugger said. "The ship has been searched thoroughly. Our mission is done. These ships will escort you the rest of the way. The passengers will be evacuated later."

"Thanks for coming to our rescue," Tony said. "Like you said, this could've been so much worse."

"No problem, happy to help." Rugger knelt down to address George and Grace. "Besides, it was worth it to meet these two." He stroked George's head.

June smiled, "Scratch is chin."

Rugger raised his eyebrows, but complied. George held his head up and closed his eyes. Obviously enjoying his chin scratch. "Well, I'll be. He likes it."

"Penguins in captivity seem to adjust well to human companionship. Many seem to enjoy it. These two are no exception."

Rugger stood up. "Well, I gotta get on this last chopper. It's ready to take off. Good luck."

Everyone on the deck yelled "Thank you" and waved as Rugger boarded the chopper and departed.

The deck was silent for a few moments. They were nearing the continent. People wanted to see whatever they could before they were forced to leave. The amount of ice in the water was increasing. The icebergs were bigger now and intimidating. The wind had died down and the sun had come out, giving some of the icebergs a brilliant blue hue. The ship was sailing calmly through the water. The view was breathtaking. Lucas realized that Saif, Nadil and Suha had joined them on deck.

"Thank you, Allah," Nadil whispered. His eyes were closed, and his face was raised to the sun. Lucas closed his eyes and said a thank you to his own God. He knew the Muslim religion had different beliefs than his own. He wondered if they were praying to the same being. They each just called Him by a different name.

"Look!" a passenger yelled, pointing toward the water. A blue whale had broken the surface. A spectacular spray coming from its blowhole. At nearly 70 feet long, it took a few seconds after its head submerged before its tail broke the surface and gave a flip, as if waving hello.

"They're endangered," Tony said. "Hunting them was outlawed 59 years ago. They had been hunted so close to extinction; they are still endangered after 59 years. Struggling to survive. Mankind is not making it easy on them."

The animal was majestic. The thought of someone killing it made Lucas's stomach turn. He thought about what Tosin had said about the rhinos. It made him wonder how many animal species were endangered or near extinction. He made a mental note to look into it. Like Saif had said, it's wrong. On so many levels. He was right.

He turned to June, "Are you ready to go in?"

"Yes. I can't feel my feet."

They returned to Lucas's cabin to tuck the birds in and put on dry clothes. George and Grace had a newfound appetite. "They haven't eaten this much at once in quite a while," June said.

"Do you think they know they're almost home?"

"Yes, I do."

Chapter 15:

The Party

The dining room was busy, but not full. The mood in the air was light and happy. Lucas and June saw the Haas family at a table, including Anna. It was good to see them all together. Jakob was beaming. It seemed he was very happy to have his family together once again. Anna looked tired, but it was obvious that being with her family was just what the doctor ordered. Lucas watched them for a moment. This is the image he wanted to keep in his mind. He was trying to replace the image of Anna's pale, lifeless face with this one. They walked over to say good morning.

"Hey," Jakob stood up, extending his hand to both of them. "These are my kids, Delia and Jens. Kids, this is the man that saved your mom." The children nodded politely and said hello.

"Thanks for saving my mom," Delia said with a sincere smile.

"Yeah, thanks," Jens added. He seemed to be struggling with everything that had happened.

"Anna, how are you feeling?" June asked.

"Okay. Still weak and sore, but the doctor said I'll be fine."

Lucas turned to June. "I see the Sulimans sitting over there. Would you like to go say hello?"

"Yes."

They said goodbye to the Hass' and walked over to the Sulimans. Tosin was with them. After all, he is a Suliman. "How is everyone today?" June asked.

"Great," Suha replied. "It feels so wonderful, not being locked in a cabin, waiting to die."

"Yeah," Saif added, "we've all been locked in a cabin since we left port. Just for different reasons. You two are a big part of the reason why we can all be at this table together. We owe you."

"You don't owe us anything. Seeing you together is what we wanted and that's what we got. Debt paid." Lucas replied. June gave Lucas a kind, contemplating look. Was that a *You're right, we're good together look?*

"We're going to get something to eat. We'll see you guys later," June said.

They got their breakfast and found a table. They sat there, enjoying the serenity that comes from knowing the worst was over.

Captain Grayson entered the dining room, capturing everyone's attention. "I'm going to have breakfast with you today," he announced. "Then I'll make my announcement." The room went back to their previous meals and conversations. Captain Grayson had his breakfast at a table with Tony, Sasha and one other member of the dining staff.

When Captain Grayson had finished his meal, he walked over to greet June and Lucas. As they stood, he shook their hands. "I want to thank you both for all you have done to protect this ship and the passengers," he said. He turned to June, grinning, "I've seen the video from the deck this morning. Those birds really are something. Well done to all of you." His smile disappeared and he added, "I'm sorry about Jalal."

"I'm sorry too," Lucas said. "A lot of bad decisions that led to a life he probably never wanted. I wish we could have saved him."

"You can't save someone who isn't willing to participate in their own rescue," the captain said.

Everyone was silent as they contemplated the truth in that statement. Tony and Tosin both joined them.

"How many people have seen that video?" June asked.

"Lots," Tony replied. "I asked Mrs. Owinski where she posted it. It's already had over 1500 views. I shared the site with you. It should be on your phones. It's gonna go viral."

June was silent, still unsure how she felt about it.

"Well," the captain started, "it's time to make my announcement."

Tony turned to Lucas, June and Tosin. "I don't even know what it is yet. Sasha said I could be surprised with everyone else."

The captain positioned himself in a part of the room where he could be heard by everyone. "Ladies and Gentlemen, I promised you an announcement and an update. As many of you know, and maybe some of you don't – there was a Libyan gang on board. They were using the ship to get to Antarctica as part of a plot to take over part of the continent. They failed. Thanks to the amazing staff aboard this vessel, they didn't even come close. We lost a wonderful crew member. One of our cabin stewards, Lucia, was murdered in order for the gang to try to keep their presence on board a secret."

Lucas heard the woman from cabin 208 gasp. "Oh no, poor dear," she said quietly.

The captain continued, "It was Lucia's death that alerted us to the fact that there was at least one killer on board. It was only through the dedication and perseverance of our crew and a few passengers, that we were able to prevent them from taking control of the ship."

The room broke out in applause. Most of the passengers had no idea what had transpired since the ship left port, but they knew by the presence of the escorting ships, the choppers and the rescue team that it was very serious.

"Plus, those two saved that couple over there," a passenger yelled, pointing to Lucas and Tosin, then to Anna and Jakob. Another round of applause. Lucas and Tosin nodded politely.

Captain Grayson continued. "As many of you know, and maybe some of you don't – all passengers must be evacuated from the ship today. I apologize for having to cut your vacations short, but the ship will be heading back to Ushuaia today. We are not staying here in Antarctica. Passengers are not allowed to make the return trip aboard the ship."

A few low moans could be heard from people who were disappointed to miss out on their trip of a lifetime. "The cruise line will be contacting all of you regarding any compensation for your inconvenience. Now for the good news. I have been granted a bit of a reprieve regarding the evacuation procedures. As you can see, he said gesturing to the windows, we have officially reached Antarctica. Anyone who wants to step foot there will be allowed to do so this morning."

Another cheer from the crowd.

"You should have all received your safety briefings. The zodiacs will begin ferrying passengers soon. You will be closely monitored, and you won't be able to stay long, but at least you'll be there. Everyone must be back on board at Noon, at which time we are going to have a party here in the dining room. Since we will have no passengers returning to Ushuaia with us, we have plenty of food and beverages to spare – and we're going to enjoy it before the evacuation begins."

A mixed response from the passengers. Many of them wanted to spend more time on the continent. Most of them realized that the captain had gone out of his way just to get the approval to ferry passengers to land – and they appreciated it.

"I'm going to try to make up for last night's dinner," Sasha announced, smiling.

"Yeah, that was definitely below par," one passenger said. "Now I think I know why."

"It was necessary," Sasha replied.

"Thank you everyone for your patience and understanding," Captain Grayson said. "It has been my privilege and honor to be your captain. If you have any further questions, please reach out to a staff member."

The captain and Tony walked over to Lucas and June. "You have approval to escort George and Grace personally to El Polo Sur," he said to June. "There's a ship that will take you there, then return you to the mainland."

"Me too?" Lucas asked.

"Yes, you too," Tony answered. "I knew you would want to go so I asked the captain to get permission for you as well."

"It wasn't easy," the captain added, smiling. "I had to speak of your many heroic deeds and remind them that you are a big part of why they're not in the middle of a turf war right now."

"Thank you both so much," June replied. "I can leave right away if that's easier for the ship." She turned to Lucas. "Are you sure you want to come?"

"I'm sure. We need to talk. This trip hasn't allowed us much time for conversation."

"I would like you both to be at the party," the captain said.

Lucas crinkled his nose, "I'm not much of a party guy."

"It's important to me," the captain said.

"It's important to both of us," Tony added.

"Will there be wine?" June asked.

"Yes, of course."

June looked at Lucas, allowing him to answer. "We'll be there." Then he turned to June. "Should we go check on George and Grace?"

"Yes."

They left the dining room and headed to Lucas's cabin. They walked in silence as they replayed the events of the morning in their minds. Neither of them were in a hurry to be back in the cabin anyway.

June broke the silence. "We need to make sure we're packed so we'll be ready when it's time to depart. Then I'm going to take the birds for a walk. I don't want to sit in the cabin and I'm not taking a zodiac this morning. You're welcome to join me."

"Sounds good."

June seemed uncomfortable. "Lucas, are you sure you're okay with going to El Polo Sur? I feel like I'm keeping you from your life."

Lucas stopped in the middle of the hallway and turned to face her. June did the same. "Listen, I didn't have a life until I stepped onto this ship. Not one that I really liked, anyway. I wasn't living. I was surviving. There's a difference. I know that now. I know that because of you."

June nodded, understanding. She smiled and raised her face to his. "For the record, I really like you too." It was a perfect moment for a kiss and neither one of them were going to let that moment slip away. Lucas gazed at her face for a moment. Saving the ship. Saving the passengers. Saving the continent. It had all gotten in the way of his love life. A life he didn't even know he wanted or needed, until he did.

They entered the cabin to find a huge gift basket, complete with snacks and champagne. The card read, 'Like the captain said, we've got lots of extras. Enjoy. Signed, The Crew.'

In the room, June tended to the birds then went down the hallway to her room to pack the rest of her stuff and bring it to Lucas's room. Then they took the birds for a walk on deck. As they walked toward the stern on the port side, their eyes rested on the railing where Blade went over.

"We should ask Tony for an update, just in case."

"Agreed."

Lucas changed the subject. "That video from this morning is pretty cool. I'm glad Tony sent it to us. It's the only recording we have from this trip. Watching George and Grace slide on their bellies. That was epic. Do you think that hurt the egg?"

"No. If Grace thought it would she wouldn't have done it. I will watch her closely, just in case."

"I was thinking about nicknaming them The Dynamic Duo."

June laughed out loud. "Well, it does fit them." Then she seemed to get sad as she watched them toddle in front of her. "That's exactly who they are," she said softly.

They walked the outside deck more than once. It felt good to be outside. The weather was calm, and the sun was still shining. The scenery was spectacular. Lucas would never have believed that water and ice could be so beautiful if he wasn't standing there, seeing it for himself.

After returning George and Grace to their cage, they arrived in the dining room early. The crew was busily setting up the room for the upcoming festivities. The tables had been moved along the outer edge of the room, making an empty space in the center of the room. "Is there going to be dancing?" June asked.

"If people want to, yes," Sasha answered. "This is the best we can do considering the circumstances. I want the passengers to have a good time, even if it's only for a little while before they leave the ship. I want them to know we care. Speaking of that." Sasha walked over to a makeshift bar and poured a glass of Chardonnay, handing it to June. "Here you go. You've earned it."

"How did you know I like Chardonnay?"

"It's my job to know. Lucas, what can I get you?"

"I'm not ready for alcohol just yet."

"How about a virgin mojito?"

"Sure, if you can do that."

"I can. I have my ways." She flashed them both a mischievous smile.

"I assume you had something to do with the enormous gift basket that we found in Lucas's room. Thank you so much. It's wonderful. Is there anything we can do to help?" June asked.

"The basket was Tony's idea. I put it together. Tony delivered it. You both have done enough. Just relax and mingle."

"Any idea where Tony is?" Lucas asked.

"Probably tending to the purser duties he's had to let slide over the past 24 hours. He'll be here soon."

Elated passengers started to trickle in, fresh from their excursion to the continent. Their faces still held the looks of awe, and their eyes still sparkled with wonder from their time on land. They brought with them an infectious sense of happiness and hope.

Tony walked in. Lucas excused himself from the conversation June was having with one of the passengers to talk to Tony.

"Anything I should know?"

"Hey Lucas, good to see you. How are you doing?" Tony said in a patronizing tone. "Actually, it's fine. I'm just joking with you. But seriously, can't you just relax for a few minutes?" Tony looked at the drink in Lucas's hand. "Are you drinking?" he asked in a mock incredulous manner.

"A virgin mojito, smartass. Compliments of Sasha. It's actually pretty good."

"That's not a bad idea. I might try one."

"Tony, I'm trying to relax but I just can't shake the feeling that this isn't over yet. I feel like I don't have the right to tell myself that we won."

"I know. I feel the same way. I've jumped half out of my own skin more than once today. I keep expecting someone to come from around a corner and shoot me. It's going to take a while to get past this."

"Did they find Blade?"

"Not a trace."

"Is there any update on what June and I are supposed to do?"

"A ship is standing by to take you to the base. Later today they will bring a zodiac over to pick you up. Pretty sure they are bringing more than one. To accommodate the birds and your luggage and whatever else they load up. The captain has offered them supplies since we have so much extra."

Lucas nodded. "Thanks for the gift basket. It's huge. We already thanked Sasha."

"I hope you two get the chance to enjoy it."

"Me too."

An attendant approached them with a tray of drinks in plastic mini flute glasses. "For the toast." Lucas looked to Tony for an explanation. Tony just shrugged his shoulders. "Sasha likes to keep her plans to herself."

The dinging of silverware against a glass brought everyone's attention to the center of the room where the captain stood, holding his own mini flute. "Ladies and gentlemen, we've come to the last event of this trip and the end of our time together. Before we begin the festivities, please join me in a toast." He paused. "We lost a very dear crew member on this journey. Lucia had been a valued member of this crew for years. She was a wonderful human being. A beacon of light with an infectious smile. You couldn't help but like her. She will be dearly missed. Please raise your glasses. To Lucia."

"To Lucia!", the crowd repeated.

Lucas looked at Tony, who was trying his best to not cry. "I'm still trying to figure out what to do with the pain, the fear, the anger, all of it." Tony said. "It's all still here and I have no idea what to do with it."

"Like you said, it's going to take a while to get past this."

The captain continued, "Thank you everyone. Please enjoy the remainder of your time aboard the Ice Dancer."

Pop music started playing. The party had begun.

"Lucas," Tony began, "the captain found out that the same credit card that booked 208 also booked 321. Your cabin."

He had been hired by the gang. But why?

"I assume part of their plan required a diver, which is how Blade convinced the gang to bring Tosin. They probably decided they wanted a backup." Lucas said.

"Why would they need a diver now? I think it would be months before they would need a diver. Maybe they were going to hold you here against your will. You'd become a permanent employee."

Lucas was quiet, thinking. That scenario was entirely possible – and one he had never even considered. He had accepted the job and left for the airport so quickly that his parents had no idea where he was. If he had disappeared, they would have no idea where to begin looking for him. If they were able to track him to the Ice Dancer, the trail would probably end there. They would never know the truth. He made a mental note to contact his parents as soon as possible.

Lucas walked over to June, who was chatting with passengers. The gnawing feeling of dread that he had tried to shake earlier had returned and settled into his gut, taking up permanent residence. June turned her face to his and smiled. He raised his crooked arm to her; an offer for her to take it. She looped her arm through his and seemed happily content. The light-hearted conversation shifted to include Lucas.

Little by little, the dining room emptied as passengers left to report for evacuation. People in the dining room would watch through the windows as the zodiacs ferried them to various ships waiting to take them back to Ushuaia. June and Lucas spotted the Hass family and walked over to say goodbye before it was their turn to depart. Lucas and Jakob shook hands. Lucas could tell that Jakob was not the same man that had boarded this vessel two days ago. It seemed his priorities had changed. For the better. "Thanks for saving my wife. Thanks for everything. You did a lot more than you even realize. You helped me through a tough time just by having my back. You and June and the birds. Oh, and I want that video. Send it to Anna."

"Will do."

June and Anna hugged. Anna gave June her contact information. "Stay in touch," Anna told her. "If you don't, you'll be hearing from me."

"Deal."

Next it was time to say goodbye to the Sulimans. "What will you do now?" Lucas asked the siblings.

"I wasn't kidding when I said we were leaving Tripoli," Saif said. "All of us. We've discussed it a little. We might end up where I sent Mom and Dad. Wherever we go, it needs to be soon. We've agreed that none of us can return to our jobs or our homes. It's just too risky."

"I need to make a quick stop in Tripoli. I have a promise to keep," Tosin said.

"Then I'm going with you," Nadil offered.

"Me too," Saif added. "But I don't want to be in Tripoli any longer than necessary. Like, only a couple of hours. Do what you need to and then we're out of there."

"I told myself I would never step foot in Tripoli again. I'm not looking forward to going back. We'll make it quick."

"Where was the dagger?" Lucas asked.

"In the prayer rug. I sewed a pouch in the bottom. When it was rolled up, no one could tell it was there."

Tony joined the group. He wanted to say goodbye to the Sulimans as well. After several hugs and fond farewells, the Sulimans left to report for evacuation. Tony studied Lucas for a moment, then said, "Eluxoroma. It means growth during crisis. It fits you perfectly – and the ship going to El Polo Sur is ready when you are," Tony said.

June sighed heavily. "This is what I came for. Time to take them home." It took another ten minutes to say goodbye to various crew members and the few remaining passengers.

Chapter 16:

Arriving at El Polo Sur

They arrived at the loading area. Zodiacs had already departed with their luggage and the supplies that the captain had offered. George and Grace were there, squawking in their cage. They calmed down a bit when June and Lucas arrived.

"I'll be in the same zodiac as them, correct?" June asked, motioning to the birds.

"Yes, ma'am. The purser said that was a requirement. He said separating you from them would not be a good idea."

"He was right. Thank you."

Another zodiac had departed just before theirs, headed for the same ship. It looked empty, with just one man operating the prop motor.

"Is that one empty?" June asked.

"Lucia is on that one. She was from Argentina. The Argentina government has allowed her to be buried at the base. Her family agreed. They would prefer that she be there than in some cemetery in Argentina. I never met her, but I've been told she loved her job, and she loved Antarctica. Never got tired of the view."

June had never met Lucia, but for some reason, knowing she would be there gave her comfort.

"We're fairly close to the base, aren't we?" Lucas asked.

"Yes, sir. Your cruise ship can get close enough that you could've just been ferried in by zodiac, but the decision was made to not let it get that close. For safety's sake. We'll board the research vessel. It will be a short trip to the base. Then a short zodiac ride to shore. We'll be there soon."

George and Grace were stretching their necks, trying to see their surroundings. They were honking excitedly. As if they were saying, *Are we there yet*?

On board the research vessel, a crew member showed June where the cage would be kept for the short trip. "Don't worry ma'am, they'll be fine. You can come check on them if you like."

"I want to be on the same zodiac as them when we go to shore."

"Yes, ma'am."

Lucas had to coax her to get her to leave. "C'mon," he said "they'll be fine. It's a short trip."

They each got a cup of coffee in the small galley and found a place to sit. June was visibly shaking. She knew it was almost time to say goodbye to her friends. She was not handling it well. "I didn't think it would be this hard. I mean, I know the events of the last two days have something to do with it. Lucas, I really didn't think any of us would be alive right now. I think everything is just finally catching up to me."

"June, we did it. You did it. You got them home so they could raise their baby."

"I know it's for the best. They're just a little clingy right now because of all they've been through – and I'm having a hard time letting go."

All Lucas could do was try to comfort her. He was going to miss them, too. Terribly. He was doing his best not to let June see that. There was so much that Lucas wanted to say to her. Now didn't seem to be the right time. They sat in silence until they felt the ship stop and a crew member came in to tell them it was time to disembark. "Bundle up," he said. "Make sure you've got your gloves."

Once on land, Cruz Herrera introduced himself. After shaking his hand, June asked "Is taking these two to the penguin colony one of the first things on the list?"

"Yes, ma'am. I'd like to give these two the chance to find a spot for their new home."

"I know the penguins here don't have names, but these two do. This is George and this is Grace. Grace is carrying an egg."

"Most of the Emperor females here are as well. It's breeding season. They'll be in good company. We're going to head to the colony now. I assume you want to go as well. The ship that brought you here is waiting for you to get back on it so it can leave for the mainland. It was scheduled to leave days ago, but you know that story." Cruz continued, "We really appreciated the heads up and a chance to defend the peninsula. Argentina has put a lot into this base. We would not have gone down without a fight."

Lucas and June got into the truck that George and Grace had been loaded onto. It was a short ride to the colony. Lucas had never seen so many penguins in one place at one time. Hundreds of them. They were everywhere, and not all of them looked like George and Grace. Even though it should have seemed like pandemonium, it was fairly calm. Some were standing at their nests; some were waddling about. Some of them even seemed to be having conversations. At the Emperor colony, George and Grace waddled out of their cage.

"There you go. Your new home," Cruz said. George and Grace didn't go far. They slowly explored. It seemed like they were trying to decide if they liked this place or not. Then they walked over to June and cuddled her legs.

"Oh no," June said. "they're scared."

"They'll be fine," Cruz said. "They just need some time to adjust."

June knew these birds. She was not comfortable that they would be fine. Her mind was reeling. *They need more time. It will be much harder on them if I'm not here. I can't leave them. Not yet. I can't ask the ship to stay either. It needs to leave for the mainland. Winter is coming, fast.* "Mr. Herrera, I officially request to stay. With the permission of your government. The birds need more time to adapt. It will be best for them if I am here to help them through that. I realize the last boat to the mainland will leave without me."

Cruz was silent for several seconds, contemplating her request.

"Ask permission for me too. If she stays, I stay," Lucas said.

Now Cruz had two civilians asking to stay. This was very unprecedented. But this whole situation was unprecedented. He studied them both carefully. "If that ship leaves, you'll be here for six months with no way to get home. You'll have to wait for spring. Antarctic winters are brutal. The harsh weather could have you confined to quarters much of the time."

"We understand. We'll follow the rules," Lucas said.

"Please don't make me leave them. I don't want to put up a fight over this, but I will."

Lucas shot Cruz a *'she means it'* look.

Cruz knew very little about what had transpired over the last 48 hours. He knew there was a plan to take over their base. He knew the cruise ship had alerted the outside world to the plan. He knew two ships had been captured. He had stayed at the base, along with others, ready to defend it against anyone who tried to infiltrate it. He didn't know if there would be another takeover attempt. Lucas and June had been there. They had a lot of information that could prove useful. He would really like to have time with them to find out what happened. He looked down at George and Grace, still pressed up against June's leg. They looked scared and uncertain. Cruz sighed, coming to a decision. "I'll see what I can do."

June gave a sigh of relief. "Thank you so much. The base isn't too far. I'll stay here. I'd like to walk them around. If they know I'm staying, they may be more inclined to settle down. That way you can go ask if we can stay and come back for me in a little bit."

"I'll stay with her."

Once again Cruz was silent, thinking. Now he had two civilians who hadn't been on the continent for more than an hour wanting to be left alone, outside, in a penguin colony. "I really shouldn't leave you two out here alone."

Lucas pulled out his phone and clicked on the video Tony had sent him. "Have you seen this?" he asked, showing Cruz the video. Cruz's eyes widened. He had not seen it. He pointed to the video and then to George and Grace. "That's these two?"

"Sure is. Trust me, we'll be fine."

Now Cruz understood why they were having such a hard time separating from each other. June was right. The birds still needed her. He really didn't want them to leave. There was so much he wanted to know. "All right. I'm going back to base to make the request. I'll be back soon. Are you sure you're both comfortable staying here while I'm gone?"

"Absolutely."

Cruz got into the truck, shaking his head. *This day is not going how I thought it would.*

Once Cruz was gone, George and Grace went back to surveying their surroundings. They stayed close, but they seemed to be more comfortable that June wasn't going to leave them. June walked with them. She slowly increased the area they were covering. Soon they were at the edge of the colony. June didn't want to disturb it by walking in it if she didn't have to. She was hoping George and Grace would venture in on their own. The birds toddled around the edge of the colony for a few minutes, softly cooing and honking to each other.

"Is this the human version of 'Should we live here'?", Lucas asked.

"Pretty much. That's exactly what going in and deciding to stay will mean."

The birds slowly made their way deeper into the colony. Lucas saw them both give June a sideways glance more than once. June slowly sat down. Her way of telling them 'It's okay. I'm not going anywhere'. Lucas sat down with her and studied the colony. This was George and Grace's kin. He wanted to know more about them. They spoke softly as they watched. "Do penguins fight each other?"

"Not really. They bicker. There aren't many fights to the death among penguins. They're a close-knit society. Lucas, I have to ask again. Six months. Are you sure? This is a big decision. It's a no-brainer for me. I'm staying if they let me – and maybe if they don't."

"I'm sticking with you. We haven't had much time to talk. I mean about life and each other and what that might mean. I haven't said anything because keeping us alive was important and because I didn't want to put any pressure on you. So here it is. I wasn't planning on falling in love when I stepped onto that boat. I didn't think I was ready to go through that again. Then you sat down at the dinner table and there was a spark. A spark that has been extinguished for a long time. Then you introduced me to George and Grace. I'm pretty sure I fell in love with all three of you right then and there. Now here we are. Sitting in the most incredible place I have ever been. Watching a penguin colony go about their business. I love it. It's freezing cold and I don't even feel it. I don't want to leave George and Grace. I don't want to leave you. You're my life now. If you'll have me."

June stayed silent for several seconds, processing that information. "I'm glad you're here. I want you with me. I never would have wished for the trauma that anyone had to endure on the ship. But being here with you. Getting to stay for the winter with George and Grace. Being here when the eggs hatch. I couldn't have asked for a better outcome. Lucas, something is happening. It's not just us. It's bigger than us. I feel it."

"I know. I feel it too." He took her hand, and they managed to intertwine their gloved fingers.

George and Grace were standing still in the colony, watching them. June smiled. "Did you decide to give this place a chance?" They started to wander around. Time to meet the neighbors.

"That's it? They've moved in?"

"I think so."

Cruz pulled up a few minutes later. June got up slowly, watching the birds the whole time. They shot her an uncomfortable '*We still need you. We're not sure if we like our neighbors yet*' look. June had been their main caretaker since the day she met them. She had never seen them in the wild. This was all new to her. She was happy and sad at the same time.

June and Lucas walked back to the truck. Cruz could see the torment on her face. He understood. "So listen, here's the deal," he said. "The ship has left for the mainland. They thought you were onboard. Oops." He shrugged his shoulders. "I sent a notice that you will have to remain here for the winter. We've got plenty of supplies, thanks to Captain Grayson. We've got plenty of space, since most of the residents have left for the winter. That's my story and I'm sticking to it. Now it's your story too." *I am so getting fired for this*, he thought to himself.

"Got it," Lucas said.

"Done." June was beaming and Lucas was pretty sure he saw tears of joy in her eyes.

"They went in on their own?" Cruz asked, giving a head wave toward the colony.

"Yes. It seems they've decided to stay."

"Good. Let's let them do their thing and head back to base. I've got a lot of work to do."

June walked back toward the colony. "Say good night Gracie."

"Honk!"

Cruz looked at her in disbelief. "You gotta be kidding me."

"Nope, not kidding," June smiled – and hopped in the truck.

Cruz shot Lucas a *'You've got your hands full with that one'* look. Lucas nodded. "Tell me about it."

Chapter 17:

All Hands Lost

Back at base, Cruz pulled up in front of a brightly painted house. All the buildings at the base were painted in bright colors, making them easy to see against the rocky landscape.

"This is your place. It's empty for the winter. Your luggage is already inside. We don't hand out house keys here. No one locks their doors. Be at that building in one hour for dinner," he said, pointing to a larger red building. "That's the community center. We call it the joda. We'll eat there tonight so you can meet everyone else here."

Lucas and June thanked him and went inside. They both immediately peeled off their heavy boots and coats, which they had been wearing all day.

"That feels better," June said.

They both sank into the couch. It had been a long day. June set the alarm on her phone for 45 minutes, just in case they fell asleep. "I don't want anybody mad at us on our first day here."

Lucas dozed off quickly, but June couldn't sleep. She got up and walked around the house. She checked out the bedrooms and bathroom and kitchen. Their luggage had been set just inside the door, along with Lucas's diving gear and the huge gift basket. She thought about where to put the luggage. Should she put the luggage in one bedroom, or should she put it in separate bedrooms?

Lucas had made his feelings clear. Putting the luggage in one bedroom was an open invitation. It would come with expectations. She wasn't sure she was ready for that just yet. She put the gift basket on the dining table and left everything else where it was. She took a mental note of supplies in the kitchen. Not much here, which makes sense since the building was supposed to be empty for six months.

After June's alarm went off, they got their coats and boots on and began walking to the community center. Penguins walked freely around the base like it was a normal daily activity.

"Those are different penguins," Lucas said.

"Yes. Those are Adele penguins."

"How many kinds of penguins are there?"

"There is some argument about that. Some people say up to twenty-two. I stick with the most common identification of eighteen different species. Not all of them live in Antarctica. Some live in warm climates like Africa and Australia," she added "And a group of penguins is called a waddle."

"Makes sense, that's what they do. Are they endangered?"

"Some are. There is a breed that only lives in the Galapagos Islands. It's estimated that less than 1500 still exist – and that number keeps falling."

"Are penguins really burned instead of wood?"

"There is some argument about that, too. The story is that early explorers burned thousands of them, maybe even millions of them for heat. It is said they burn well because of the oil in their fur. One thing is certain, when man came to Antarctica to explore, many penguins and seals were slaughtered so the explorers could survive."

Cruz welcomed them at the joda. He introduced them to the other individuals who were staying for the winter. They had dinner first, since everyone was hungry. Then they were each given a two-way radio and documents with instructions on how things were done and what to expect at El Polo Sur. "We've got medical staff here, if needed. There's a military presence, too. Any unnecessary buildings will be closed for the winter. We try to get together as much as possible, to exchange information and for the socialization. We have a tradition of pizza here on Saturday nights. We try to keep that going during the winter, weather permitting. It's important not to stay isolated in your quarters for six months. That makes it too easy to forget why we're here. I'll expect you two to participate."

"Absolutely," June said. I'd like to study all the penguins here as much as possible, with your permission. I never expected to get the opportunity to watch them in their natural habitat. I'd like to make the most of it. Weather permitting, of course."

"I thought you might. This is Thom. He's our penguin specialist. He's happy to include you in his research and be your mentor. He's the boss. You follow his instructions."

"Understood."

Cruz continued, "I want to know everything that happened on your ship. Everyone here would like to know. We have very little information on what actually happened or if another attempt at a land grab is a possibility. Any information you can give us could prove useful at some point. We can have that discussion tomorrow. It's been a long day. We got together some food and supplies for you. I figured there wouldn't be much at your quarters. All living quarters need to be well-stocked in case a storm keeps us confined to quarters at some point." Cruz continued, "The weather is supposed to tolerable for the next few days. We're entering winter, so it could get very bad very quickly. We'll meet here tomorrow for lunch. Thom will be making a few trips to the colonies tomorrow. He can take you with him."

"I'll pick up you at 7am," Thom said.

"What should I do?" Lucas asked.

"There's plenty to do. I'm going to put you to work. Everything needs to be maintained here and kept in working order, like the generators. Without them, we'll probably freeze to death." Cruz answered. "But before you go, show the group the video you showed me earlier. They're not going to believe it."

The next morning Thom was outside of their quarters promptly at seven. June hopped in the truck, anxious to study the different species that call this place home. Not just penguins. She said good morning and commented how grateful she was that they had coffee and how happy she was to find a travel mug in the kitchen so she could bring it with her. "Thank you so much for letting me join you. I'm so excited."

"You're welcome. It's nice to have people here who are excited about this place. We always get people here in the summer who have never been here before, but winters can get boring. I'm looking forward to having a penguin study partner. I don't usually visit the Emperors first, but I figured you'd be anxious to check on your birds. I'm really looking forward to meeting them."

"I am a bit anxious. I couldn't help but get visions of them out here overnight, suffering. It was hard to leave them. I kept getting up and looking out the window. Part of me still doesn't believe I'm here."

"We're happy to have you. When Cruz had to decide about whether you could stay or not, he asked a few of the people here. We agreed with him. We've got the space. We've got enough supplies. From what we've been told, you and Lucas have proven yourselves to be smart and capable and trustworthy. Most of us feel you're here for a reason. It just felt wrong to send you away."

They spent the morning visiting the different colonies. At the Emperor colony, George and Grace waddled right over to June as soon as they saw her. Thom was impressed at the strong bond that had been forged during their time together. They seemed to be adapting well to being back in the wild.

"I don't get to see that kind of behavior here. I don't see how their behavior changes when they grow attachments to humans from being in captivity. This is a learning experience for me too."

Everything seemed normal at the Adele and Gentoo colonies. They saw seals, too. June asked a lot of questions. Thom spent a lot of time answering them. Then they headed back to base for lunch. Thom dropped June off at their quarters. Lucas was there. It looked like he had just gotten back as well. June was surprised at how happy she was to see him. She had loved every minute of the morning. Learning about the wildlife there. Now she realized how happy she was that Lucas was there with her.

Cruz wasn't there when they arrived for lunch. They talked with the other residents, learning their stories and more about their roles at the base. Everyone had sat down with their food when Cruz walked in. His face was ashen. This wasn't good.

Shit.

June felt panic setting in. Whatever it was, she didn't want to hear it. No more bad news. Lucas sighed heavily. He felt it, too. The rest of the group seemed apprehensive and confused. They did not yet understand what had happened on that ship.

Cruz took a deep breath. "The Ice Dancer has gone down. All hands appear to be lost."

"No. No!" June said. She turned to Lucas. "I can't do this. I need air." She walked out of the building.

Lucas found her outside, pacing like a caged animal. "Tony, Sasha, Captain Grayson. All of them." She looked at Lucas with fire in her eyes. Her flight mode out of the building had transitioned to fight mode. "If I ever get my hands on who did this." She didn't finish the thought. She didn't need to.

Lucas felt the same way, but he knew he couldn't fuel June's rage by adding his own. He let her continue to pace until he saw her stance change. Her pace slowed; her shoulders fell. The grief was setting in.

He wrapped his arms around her. "We don't know what caused it to go down."

She buried her face in his coat and sobbed. Acceptance.

After a few minutes Cruz came out. "We need to know what you know. When you're ready, come inside and tell us everything."

Once Cruz went back inside, June looked at Lucas "Should we tell them who Tosin really is?"

"No. He boarded the ship as Sulieman. That's all they need to know. We have to respect his privacy and protect his identity." June nodded.

Back inside the joda, Lucas and June sat down and squared their shoulders. They were going to relive the past three days. Was it really the past three days? It felt like it had all happened months ago. Lucas realized that the passengers probably hadn't even made it back to Ushuaia yet. "What do you know about the ships that took the passengers back to the mainland? Do you know if they're all safe?" Lucas asked, to no one in particular.

Cruz answered. "I know the Argentinian vessels are safe. They haven't reached Ushuaia yet. There were a lot of vessels from different countries and none of them could accommodate all the passengers. Things got pretty hectic. I don't even know which passengers ended up on which boats. I do know that every ship had a copy of the ship's manifest so they could identify which passengers they ended up with."

"Do you know what happened to the Ice Dancer? Why it went down?" Lucas asked.

"No. All I know is that it went down quickly." Cruz added.

Lucas looked at the floor. He was about to tell the story of how the crew of the Ice Dancer did amazing things and saved the passengers; but in the end they couldn't save themselves. June could feel the weight on his shoulders. She took his hand. This was his story to tell. Lucas started, "Everything seemed fine on the day we left port. It wasn't until the next day when Lucia's body was found that we knew something was wrong." He spent the next hour recounting the events as best he could and answering questions. The people here were trying to understand exactly what happened. He knew that. He knew it was important for them to understand. June occasionally added details. She explained how she knocked out Moose and got Suha out of the cabin. They omitted the fact that the Suliman's knew Tosin and that Sulieman was Tosin.

Lucas showed them the video again. He identified Blade and Jakob and pointed out that Blade had a knife pointing at Jakob that you can't see in the video. Yesterday when the group watched that video they laughed. Today they didn't.

"You just can't make this stuff up." someone said.

"Who would want to." another person added.

Lucas looked at Cruz, "How's the internet service here?"

"We have it. Some days are better than others. During a storm, not so good. We do our best to keep it working."

"Do you have a copy of the ship's manifest?"

"I do."

"Can I have it? I have a lot of questions I need to try to find answers to."

"Not yet. That's not something I should be handing out. I know why you're asking, and I think you should have it. I need to check on that first. I'm not sure I'm ready to rack up more reasons to get myself fired just yet."

June looked at Thom. "Can we go check on the colonies?"

"Sure. I was going to do another run today anyway."

"I'm coming too, if that's okay." Lucas added.

"Absolutely."

At the Emperor colony, George and Grace saw June approach. They paused before they quickly waddled up to her. They cuddled her legs, looking up at her with comforting eyes. June sat down and began to sob. They stayed close, cooing softly.

"They know," Thom said.

"Yeah," Lucas replied.

They waited until June's sobs subsided and she regained her composure before they approached. Lucas needed some time with the birds as well. He was having his own issues adapting to the fact that they were back in the wild. George and Grace were happy to see him. They toddled up to him and enjoyed getting petted.

Thom squatted down to say hello. He felt it was time to officially introduce himself. "You two are very special." he said to them softly.

As they prepared to leave, June said "Say good night, Gracie."

"Honk!"

"Thanks, girl. I really needed that right now. Be safe. I can't lose you two. I just can't."

Thom dropped Lucas and June off at their house. "We're not having dinner at the joda tonight. Everyone needs time to process the events of the last few days. You guys have a good night. See you tomorrow."

Chapter 18:

Saying Goodbye

They took advantage of their free time by sending emails to their parents. June hadn't talked to her parents since she was in Ushuaia. Lucas hadn't talked to his since before he left for the airport. The internet connection was good enough to get them online. June sent emails to Anna and Suha as well. She hoped she would get responses soon. She was anxious to know that everyone was okay. She knew she would have trouble sleeping; even though her brain hurt, and her body felt like lead. They both pushed themselves to exhaustion. Neither one of them were ready to close their eyes. The ship going down had been playing in their heads all afternoon. They couldn't help it. They couldn't stop it. They didn't want to live that nightmare in their dreams.

They had slept in separate bedrooms the night before. Lucas had suggested it. June knew he was trying to be a gentleman, and she appreciated it.

"Can we sleep in the same room tonight? Please," June asked.

"Of course."

"I'm going to go lay down. I don't even have the energy or ambition to change my clothes."

Lucas shut down his laptop. "Okay, but a shower first thing in the morning." He gave her a mischievous smile.

She smiled weakly. She appreciated his attempt to lighten the mood. They had been walking around the house like zombies for hours. She glanced over at the gift basket sitting on the dining table. Tony had put it in Lucas's cabin. *Someday, we will open that basket and toast you all.*

Once they were in bed and June was in Lucas's arms, she went right to sleep.

Thom arrived at 9am the next morning. "I figured you both could use some extra time today."

"Thanks," June said. "It was a rough night. Neither one of us slept well. I had a dream about the ship going down. Sat bolt upright in bed. It took a few seconds before I realized where I was. I'm glad Lucas was there." She gave him a loving look and put her gloved hand in his.

Before heading to the colonies, Thom dropped Lucas off so he could help with some tasks that needed to be done. "We're having a memorial service today. Then lunch at the joda. We were going to bury Lucia yesterday. After learning about the Ice Dancer, we decided to wait until today."

"Okay. See you soon." Lucas answered as he hopped out of the truck.

June enjoyed the distraction that visiting the colonies provided. She pushed her mind back into research mode, paying attention to everything Thom showed her. George and Grace looked up when she approached. She gave them the best smile she could muster. They watched her for a moment and chose to stay at their nest. Their look seemed to say, *We're here if you need us.* Part of her wanted them to rush to her every time she visited, but she knew they needed to be fine on their own – and so did she.

Back at base they went straight to the cemetery. Most of the residents were already there, including Lucas and Cruz. The grave had already been dug. The ground was not yet frozen. Cruz gave a wonderful eulogy. It was obvious he had taken the time to learn about Lucia. He talked about her family and her passions. One of the residents recorded the whole thing so it could be sent to her family. Cruz also gave a eulogy for the lost crew members. He mentioned every crew member by name, including their title and position aboard the ship. Lucas and June did their best to allow the ceremony to give them a sense of closure. They did not want to fall back into the black hole that had consumed them the night before.

Lunch was treated like a wake. They used supplies from the Ice Dancer, including fish and napkins with the ship's emblem on them. Photos of Lucia were displayed, along with a photo of everyone in the crew. The mood was light. Conversations varied among the residents. Many people were still asking Lucas and June for clarification on the story they had told the day before. Lucas and June asked them for clarification on how things were done at the base and what they could expect over the next six months. Lucas asked if he could get the full crew list.

"Sure." Cruz answered. "I have no problem giving you that."

"Thanks. I have so many questions; and no idea where to start looking for answers."

Everyone took a small plastic flute glass to toast the lives lost. Cruz asked Lucas if he would give the toast. "I really think this one should come from you."

Lucas nodded. He couldn't refuse. That would feel like a snub to the people he had grown to think of as friends. He had to do it. For them.

A clinking of silverware against glass silenced the room. Lucas started. "A few days ago, I boarded the Ice Dancer. I had been a loner for years, keeping to myself. I had never been on a cruise before. I felt very much out of place. Forty-eight hours later, I was in love with this beautiful woman and two amazing penguins. I ended up in the Southern Ocean, trying to save a pompous ass and the wife I didn't feel he deserved. I was helping the crew try to figure out why

109

one of their own was dead. I made friends. People that I barely knew, but I knew I could trust them with my life. Something like that changes you. It changed me. They changed me. You have all heard the story of what happened on that ship. You all know how amazing the people we honor today really were. I wouldn't be standing here now if it wasn't for them and what they did to protect us. They deserved so much. So much more than this. I will honor and respect them for the rest of my life. I pray that you will do the same." Lucas raised his glass. "To the crew of the Ice Dancer."

"To the crew of the Ice Dancer." the group responded.

After the toast Lucas joined June, and they continued to mingle with the residents. Wine and beer from the ship had been set up in the room. June's eyes rested on the Chardonnay. The same brand that Sasha had poured for her two days earlier.

"Would you like a glass?" the resident bartender asked.

"Yes, please."

Lucas saw June's hands shake as she took the glass. She looked at him with tears in her eyes. "I miss them so much."

"Me too." He raised his arm, elbow extended. A warm smile on his face. She smiled as she accepted his invitation, looping her arm through his.

One by one, residents left to get back to their daily tasks. Lucas and June stayed and helped clean up. It was time to start acting like members of the team. There was so much they needed to learn about the place that was now their temporary home. These people had taken them in and accepted them as one of their own. They wanted to show their respect and appreciation. Besides, it was good to focus on something else for a while.

Back at their quarters, Lucas began looking up the crew members online. He asked June to help. "I want to find as many social media accounts for the crew as I can, and I know very little about social media."

They were able to find social media accounts for most of the crew on either Facebook, Instagram, X or Snapchat. They even found some videos on YouTube. They spent hours poring over the platforms, learning so much about the friends they had lost. Some of the crew were very creative and had posted some pretty funny stuff. Soon Lucas and June were laughing hysterically. They learned about Sasha's life all the way back to when she started cooking school. They found social media accounts for the Haas's and the Sulieman's, but nothing for Tosin.

June got up, standing between Lucas and the dining table. "Should we open the gift basket?"

"Sure."

"Tony brought that to your cabin. I think opening it should be special."

"I think I'm ready. Are you?"

"Yes."

They poured champagne into a couple of drinking glasses that they found in the cupboard and sat back down at the laptop. The monitor showed a picture with most of the crew, smiling.

June raised her glass to the monitor. "Thank you for everything."

Lucas raised his glass. "I'm going to figure this out." he said to the people in the photo.

June turned to Lucas. "I realize I don't know how I would have gotten through the past few days without you. You are the most amazing person I have ever met. I'm not trying to be pushy, but if you love me, I consider myself the luckiest girl in the world. And I really want to kiss you."

Lucas's expression turned into one of love and joy and admiration. "I thought you'd never ask – and I do love you."

At that moment for June, Lucas Kalloe became the only person in the world. Her face moved close to his. Her hair brushing his cheeks. She brushed the end of his nose with hers. Their first kiss was soft and safe. Testing the waters. Their second kiss was stronger. Two people committing completely to whatever path lay ahead. Their third kiss erupted in a fury of passion that resulted in Lucas carrying her to the bedroom and the prompt removal of clothing. She was a virtual treasure map. Every inch a new bit of treasure he never thought he would find. From her hair to her toes and everything in between. Nothing was off limits. He loved the sounds she made. Kiss her here, a low moan. Touch her there, a squeal of passion. It was music to him. He loved exploring every nook and cranny. Forehead, nose, ears, lips, belly button, knee, toes. He wanted her to know that there wasn't anything about her body that he didn't love. Not even that one toe that was slightly out of proportion with the rest. That toe was perfect.

Chapter 19:

Looking For Clues

Lucas awoke in the morning with his arms around her. His face buried in her hair. He needed to pee. He slowly pulled himself away.

"Good morning.", she mumbled.

"Good morning. I'll be right back."

When he returned, she had rolled over so she was now facing him. Tousled hair and smudged mascara. She was still beautiful. He wanted her again, and she knew it.

"I need to pee and take a shower first. I'll make it quick."

"Ok Speedy Gonzales."

Lucas took his shower next. When he came out of the bathroom, she was lying on the bed with a very inviting look. He was happy to oblige. He crawled onto the bed and hovered over her. He kissed her neck softly, then met her gaze. "You, Junebug" he paused, kissing her neck again, "are absolutely delicious."

"Good to know." she said, wrapping her arms around his neck and her legs around his torso.

About an hour later Lucas's radio beeped. It was Cruz. "We've got strong winds coming in so stay in your quarters. If the winds die down enough to go check on the colonies later, Thom will contact you."

The internet was working well enough for them to check their emails and continue to scour the internet for clues. June received a reply from Anna. All was well. They made it back to Ushuaia and were headed home to Austria. She had a reply from her parents who were very happy to hear from her. They had been doing their best to get updates on the Ice Dancer and they knew something was wrong, particularly when typing "Ice Dancer" into the Google search box brought up a top result of a video of their daughter sliding down the deck of the ship with George and Grace and a stranger.

June relayed all of this to Lucas. "Look what I found." Lucas said. "I found pictures that the crew posted the day we left port. Look in the background." Lucas did his best to zoom in on the background. June moved her face closer to the monitor, peering at the now grainy photo. "Is that Blade?"

"I think so."

"I don't recognize who he's talking to."

"Me either. I wonder if Tosin will recognize him. Have you heard from Suha yet?"

"No. I'm not worried though. They have a lot to deal with right now. Lucas, we need to stop calling him Tosin."

"You're right. If we don't, we might make a mistake and give his identity away," Lucas sighed. "I met him as Sulieman. Then I knew him as Tosin. Now I have to go back to calling him Sulieman."

The quiet day gave them the chance to talk about things they needed to talk about. About each other.

"Lucas, have you ever been in love?"

"Yes, once."

"What was her name?"

"Maria."

"Will you tell me about her?"

"Yes. We met in Rio De Janeiro through mutual friends. Our first date was dinner at a restaurant. It's a good choice because it gives you time to get to know the person. It also gives you a chance to end the date after dinner if things aren't going so well. We got along just fine. Soon after that our dates were mostly going out with our friends. We were young and Rio can be quite the party town if you know where to go. I had recently moved to Rio. I didn't have many friends. Being with Maria and making new friends felt good. We moved in together. Just as I was getting used to that life, it was all taken away. I took a diving job that required me to travel. I was gone for a few days. Maria went out with her friends while I was away. She was killed by a drunk driver. Her friends told me later she didn't even drink that night. She knew she had to drive home. She just didn't want to sit home by herself. She wanted to be out with people; and one of those people killed her. Suddenly my life made no sense. I couldn't focus so I couldn't take any jobs. I was a mess. Diving was too big of a risk. So, I sat home and retreated into my shell. Trying to figure out the answers to questions I will never have answers to. Our friends came by to keep me company and try to cheer me up. They would encourage me to get out of the house. For months I rarely left the house. Eventually they stopped coming around. They had to get back to their lives. I understood. I didn't like feeling like a burden or an obligation. I told them I'd be fine, and I would see them once I got my head together. I had been saving money for a ring. It just seemed like the next logical step. I used that money to bury her. Shortly after that I moved to Barra Mansa. I needed to get away from Rio. I'm not going to lie to you. I miss her. Part of me always will. When I lost her, a piece of my soul went with her. That part of me is with her now. I can't give it to anyone else. I never believed in love at first sight. I thought it was something romance novelists made up to sell more books. Until I met you. That's never happened to me before. Maria and I didn't fall in love that way. The moment I saw you, I felt more alive than I have in a long time. Like a dormant seed had just sprouted. A part I thought would be dead forever. A new piece of my soul. That part of me is yours." He paused. "You can have the rest of me too," he grinned. "How about you? Any ridiculously handsome former boyfriends that I should know about? The jealous type?"

"No. I don't think so. I had a few boyfriends. Even lived with one of them for a while. None of them were particularly serious. Looking back, I think I kept them at a distance because somewhere in the back of my mind, I knew I didn't want to stay in New York. It was after the last relationship ended that I registered for the bird fair. I knew it was time to move on and I needed to do something to make that happen. I'm glad I did. Eventually it led me to you."

"And George and Grace."

"And George and Grace." June repeated.

"I really like those birds." Lucas said. "When will the egg hatch?"

"Probably end of May or early June. She'll lay the egg before then. It takes about two months after that before it hatches. Grace will go off to feed and leave the egg with George. She'll come back to feed the chick."

"You mean throw up food for the baby?" Lucas grimaced.

"Yes. That's how they feed their young. Gross, but effective."

"Do you think we'll get to see it hatch?"

"It would be a miracle if we got to witness it hatching. Come July there will be lots of Emperor babies. This trip has been one miracle after another. I'm hoping for another one."

"Will the Adele and Gentoo penguins have their babies as well?"

"No. Only Emperor chicks are born in the winter."

"Will the babies be in danger?"

"Yes. They'll be defenseless so predators will be looking to score an easy meal. They won't have the insulation that the adults have so they could freeze to death. They can't swim when they're young so if they end up in the water, they drown. They take their first swim at about five months old. That's when they're old enough to be on their own and the parents will stop caring for them.. If the ice that the colony is located on collapses before they can swim, they will end up in the water. That has happened recently. Thousands of chicks drowned. Changes in their environment is a big factor in their dwindling numbers."

Later in the day Thom contacted them to see if they wanted to make a run to check on the colonies. The wind had calmed down enough to make the trip. Twenty minutes later, two trucks pulled up. As Lucas and June came outside, Thom got out of one truck and Cruz got out of another. "It's time you two had a vehicle," Cruz said. "I had a couple of guys give this a tune-up to make sure it would run for you."

"Thanks." Lucas said. "We'll only use it if we need to. It's not like we can go shopping or anything."

The four of them made the rounds to check on the colonies. George and Grace were hunkered down in their spot. They acknowledged June when they saw her but did not leave their nest. When they prepared to leave June said, "Say good night Gracie."

"Honk!"

"That never gets old," Thom said. "I need to record that. It will go viral like the video from the ship."

"One day I won't be able to do that, so I'm going to do it every chance I get. That's a great idea. I would like to have a video of that to remember them by."

"We'll do it next time we're here. Before we get too far into winter when there's only four hours of daylight."

Chapter 20:

Finding A Purpose

Saturday nights at the joda were a welcome affair. There was usually pizza for dinner. After working and seeing the same few people all week, it was refreshing to be able to visit and socialize with the rest of the residents. Announcements regarding the base and work to be done were made early, so people could enjoy the rest of their evening. Some people sat and talked. Some people played games. Birthdays were celebrated. The mood was always light and festive.

George and Grace were often a topic of discussion. El Polo Sur did, after all, have two famous penguins as permanent residents. Everyone at the base had taken turns accompanying Thom and June to the evening visit to the Emperor colony. Lucas came if he didn't have work to do. June started letting other residents say, "Say good night Gracie." Every time Grace honked in response. The residents loved it. Not to be outdone, several other penguins decided to join in on the action and began honking along with Grace. Thom had taken a video when it was just Grace saying good night. Then he took another video when a few more joined in. Now there were over a dozen penguins honking good night right on cue.

The subject of penguins brought about the upcoming arrival of the Emperor babies. That discussion transitioned into the well-being of the colony to ensure the best chance of survival for the hatchlings, which led to the well-being of the continent as a whole. There were many opinions on what was best for Antarctica and the consequences of mankind's presence there. Most people agreed that humans were now looking at the continent as a money-making opportunity. "People are trying to figure out how they can exploit this place for profit," one person said. "Russia and Libya aren't the only ones trying to figure out how to get rich here."

Another resident added, "It should be Antarctica first. Its well-being should get top priority. That's how it's supposed to be. Mankind's presence here is supposed to be minimal. Research only. That priority is shifting. Profit is becoming a higher priority than what's best for the land. Jets are now landing directly on the ice to bring tourists."

"All that weight. All that heat. All that carbon dioxide spewed into the atmosphere. That can't be what's best for the environment here." Lucas said.

"And yet, it happens all summer long. Rules are being bent. Soon they will be broken – and so will the continent."

Lucas could see the look of pain on June's face. The penguins, the seals, this amazing place. All in danger so people could make money. His head was spinning. Thoughts were forming in his mind faster than he could sort them out. Things were coming full circle for him. It was all starting to make sense. He got up to find a quiet place to think. A few minutes later June joined him. "Are you okay?" she asked. "You looked like you needed a few minutes alone."

Lucas turned to her, his eyes wide with excitement and hope. This was not the look she was expecting. She expected to find him stressed and pacing. Instead, he looked like a kid on Christmas morning. "I know why I'm here," he said slowly. The next few minutes were a whirlwind as Lucas tried to put everything that had been swirling in his mind into words. He spoke quickly as his thoughts poured out, one after the other.

"My whole life I never had a real purpose. At least not one that I considered significant. Born in a small country, grew up and became a diver. That's pretty much it. I thought I would just marry Maria, and we would go about living our lives. You know; go to work, have kids, buy groceries. Maybe get a dog. Boring, everyday stuff. I was okay with that. I considered that a good life. I was naive. I didn't know any better. Then I stepped onto that ship. I knew why I was there, but I didn't really know. You know what I mean? I was hired to do a job. A job that I never did. Heck, I don't even know if there was an actual job for me to do. Then I met you and George and Grace." He put his hands on both sides of her face. "You. You wonderful you. Then all hell broke loose, and I had to protect you. Protect all of you. Suddenly I had something to fight for. Something to live for. I didn't even think about it at the time. Things happened so quickly that I just did what needed to be done. I just reacted and went on to the next task. Now we're here. In this amazing place. We weren't supposed to spend the winter in Antarctica together. Or were we? Because here we are. George and Grace are going to have a baby. We get to be part of that. There's a video out there of us sliding down the deck of the ship. Maybe millions of people have seen it by now. People are paying attention. People are taking notice. We did that. Without even trying. I didn't know anything about this place a month ago. I've learned so much. There are plenty of people who want to profit from it. Antarctica needs people to fight for it. That's what I'm supposed to do." He moved his hands to her shoulders and squeezed them gently. "June, *I know*."

June gazed at him with a look of pride and admiration. Her look said, *You wonderful man, you.* "Not without me. I'm in."

Lucas did a spin on the ball of one foot. Then he scooped June up and spun her around. "Why am I so happy?" he asked. June chuckled.

"What?"

"I couldn't help it," she said. "It just popped into my head. I wonder if Noah was this happy when he was told he had to build an ark." Lucas just smiled and kissed her. Then he pulled away, a frown on his face. "What if we fail?"

"If this is what we're supposed to do. We won't fail. People will help us."

Lucas's dark eyes sparkled and he smiled. "They will. We have friends."

They walked back into the main area of the joda. The group they had been talking to earlier were still sitting at the table. Thom had joined them. "We need some help," June announced.

"Sure. What's up?"

"We'd like a list of every person, group or organization that you know of that cares more about protecting this place than exploiting it. We already know this base is one of them. I haven't seen any indication that this base is willing to exploit the land for profit. I realize we can find a lot of this information online, but we want your personal input. Your opinion means a lot."

Thom smiled, "Sounds like you two are ready to stand up and be heard."

"Yep."

"I knew you were here for a reason. I want in." Thom volunteering himself was quickly followed by voices from the rest of the group.

"Count me in."

"I'm down with that."

"Let's do this."

"Finally!"

June turned to Lucas with a look of satisfaction. He just smiled at her, *You wonderful you.*

Chapter 21:

We're Not Alone

Grace laid her egg in early June, along with other females at the colony. One day when the weather conditions were good enough for June and Thom to come for a visit, Grace was waddling about and George stayed in the nest, steadfast and stoic. It was the first time June ventured into the colony. She suspected that George was sitting on the egg, but she had to be sure – and she just had to see it for herself. George seemed happy to see her. He even leaned back a bit to briefly expose the egg so June could see it. He looked like such a proud papa. Grace waddled around them, honking. She seemed to be saying that it was time for her to go. June walked out of the colony with tears in her eyes. She knew the next time she came to the colony that Grace would be gone; and she wouldn't be back for over a month. She quietly prayed, "Please God, keep her safe and let her come back."

"Grace hasn't left yet to go feed," June said.. "I can tell there are a lot less penguins here. Most of the females are gone."

"She was waiting to see you before she left. I'd bet money on it," Thom said.

"You think so?"

"Yes. She needs to know you'll be here for her family. There's still some dependency there."

"I'm going to miss her so much."

"You ready to go?"

"Yes," June said slowly. "This will be the last time until she comes back."

"I know. She'll be back. Grace and George are the smartest and most capable penguins I've ever met. She'll be fine."

June walked to the edge of the colony. While chocking back her tears, she said "Say good-night Gracie."

"Honk!"

"Thank you for staying so I could say good-bye." She looked at George, sitting stoically on the egg. "I'll be back soon George. Stay safe and take care of that baby."

The brutal Antarctic winter made it impossible to visit the colony as often as June would have liked. She wanted to check on George every day, but pop up storms and high winds made it difficult. One day when the weather was fair, June hopped into the truck to make a quick visit to the colony. It was almost spring. The eggs would be hatching soon, and June was ancy. Thom wasn't available and Lucas was helping with maintenance. Thom and Cruz had told her to never visit the colonies alone. Never leave the base alone. It's too dangerous. There's no 911 service in Antarctica. *I'll just go check on George quickly*, June thought. *I haven't checked on him in days and the weather has been horrid. I need to know he's okay. I've done this a hundred times. It'll be fine.*

At the colony George was at his post, sitting on the egg. His head was down. He didn't even look up when June arrived. The males had huddled together for warmth to survive the frigid weather. The ground was covered in ice, built up over the winter. June walked deftly into the colony. George hadn't moved and she needed to know he was okay. When she approached, he looked up and gave a soft honk. She felt like he was saying, *Is it spring yet*? "Soon George," she said softly. "It will be spring soon. Your egg will hatch, and Grace will come back. Things will get better soon."

As if on cue, a strong gust of wind swept over the colony. Very strong. It blew June off her feet, and straight towards the water. She looked around for something to grab onto. Nothing. She slammed her fists onto the ice, hoping somehow, she could stop herself. It was too thick. She had no way to stop. She slid toward the water, arms flailing. Just before she slid off the ice and into the water; something – or someone, stopped her from behind. She turned with a smile on her face and the words "My hero" on the tip of her tongue. She expected to see Lucas. Except it wasn't Lucas.

Blade.

He was dirty and disheveled and gaunt. He had lost a lot of weight. He looked like he had aged ten years since the last time June had seen him. She barely recognized him. The evil grin, however, was exactly the same. Sheer terror swept over her. She was alone, and at Blade's mercy.

"Surprise," he sneered.

June stayed silent. She remembered how quick Blade was to anger. She also remembered how well Sam could read his expressions. Blade did not look happy. She needed to know what his frame of mind was. One thing she knew is that Blade liked to talk. She hoped he would tell her.

"Surprised to see me? You've probably got a lot of questions."

"I do. It's good to see you alive. Thanks for saving me."

Blade smiled. The smile was less of a sneer and almost genuine.

"You're valuable. I can use you." He pulled on her arm, and she stood up. He gave a head wave toward the penguins. "Those birds are the reason I ended up in the water. I don't know which ones are yours. I should just kill them all. But not yet. I need to break you first. By the way, I had a few of their friends for dinner. They're not bad."

June kept her expression cold and neutral. He hadn't seen her talking to George. She knew he was digging for information and trying to manipulate her. She refused to look at the birds. She knew her eyes would go straight to George. Then Blade would know.

Blade gave a hint of frustration. She wasn't playing his game. He started walking her toward the truck. He continued, "I really was ready to die. But that's not how it turned out."

"We would have saved you."

"I know. You could've let go and sent me into the water yourself. You didn't."

"I don't treat people like that." She looked him straight in the eyes, "Not even you."

His expression softened, just a little. That little bit of compassion made a difference. Good to know. June's radio was on the seat inside the truck. As Blade pushed her in, Lucas's voice came over the radio. "June, are you there? Answer me please. I need to know you're okay." Blade grabbed it and quickly turned it off. "That may be the last time you ever hear lover boy's voice."

June's mind was swirling with questions that she refused to ask. How did he survive? How did he make it to land? Where has he been hiding? She knew there were a lot of bases on the peninsula that were vacant for the winter. But how did he get there?

Back at the base, Lucas walked toward his quarters and noticed the truck wasn't there. Odd, he thought. He went into the house. June wasn't there. He walked back outside. He asked everybody he saw if they had seen June leave in the truck. No one had. If she had left, he knew exactly where she went. He was a little irritated. She knew better. He tried calling her on his radio. No response.

As he walked around the base, he saw two soldiers walking with someone. He knew them. That was Hugo and Milenka. They were on either side of the person, acting like escorts. It looked like a female, but he didn't recognize her. Not at first. As he got closer, pure elation swept over him. Sasha! She survived. If she survived maybe others did too. Before he could say anything, he realized she was not smiling. She was not happy to see him. She was handcuffed.

Shit.

Thom and Cruz approached. Lucas looked at the men, questioning. Milenka explained, "Found her hiding out at a base nearby. We started seeing indications that someone was around that we didn't know about. We knew something was up. We started searching and found two sets of footprints at some of the vacant research stations. Those stations had been broken into. Haven't found anyone else yet."

Sasha stared at the ground, refusing to speak. She was dirty and disheveled and gaunt. She had lost a lot of weight. Lucas tried to process it. Something was wrong. If she survived the ship going down, why didn't she come straight to the residents and ask for help? Why did she hide? There was someone else. Who? Someone who didn't want to be found. What the hell was going on? One thing came to Lucas's mind crystal clear. He looked up at the men, panic in his eyes. "June. She went to the colony. Alone!"

Thom broke into a sprint, headed for his truck. "Let's go!". Lucas was right behind him. Cruz took Sasha's arm. "I've got her," he said to the soldiers. "Go with them."

At the colony, there was no June and no truck. Only penguins. George was at the nest. He started honking frantically as soon as the men approached. "Something's wrong. Something happened. George knows."

"We need to start searching," Thom said. "If we're lucky, we'll be able to follow the truck tracks."

George was rocking side to side in the nest, lightly stamping his feet, honking the whole time. It was obvious he wanted to help. "George probably knows which way they went, but he can't leave the egg." Just then they heard a familiar honk, coming from behind them. They turned to see Grace waddle onto the ice, coming from the water.

"Do you think she knows June is in trouble?" Thom asked.

"Yeah, I do."

Grace went straight to the nest, honking at George. They seemed to be having a conversation. George backed off the egg and Grace immediately stood over it, taking over incubator duty. George paused and looked at the men. He seemed to be saying *Watch me.*

He took a few steps forward and plopped onto his belly, sliding right into Lucas's legs. The contact wasn't enough to knock Lucas over. Then George stood and looked up. It looked like he was saying, *Do you understand?*

Lucas felt nauseous. The video from the ship played in his mind. Is that what George was trying to tell him? That it was the man that he knocked down on the ship?

The men stared at Lucas. They had all seen the video and they all had the same thought.

"Do you think?" Thom asked, to no one in particular.

"If Sasha is here, Blade could be too. Right now, nothing would surprise me." Hugo said.

"He went into the ocean," Lucas said, shaking his head. "They never found him."

"Exactly. They never found him," Hugo replied. "If Sasha was helping him, that would explain a lot."

George promptly started waddling toward the truck, honking his instructions, *Let's go find June!*

"Those two will never cease to amaze me," Thom said.

There were enough tracks in the snow to keep the men on track most of the time. Occasionally they would lose the tracks where the wind had blown snow over them. As long as they stayed on track, George was calm. If they started to go in the wrong direction, George would honk and flail his flippers, *Not that way*!

George's demeanor soon changed. He started honking softly and anxiously. "Thom slow down."

"There's a vacant research station nearby," Thom said. They approached slowly, keeping the truck at a crawl until the station came into view. The truck was parked outside.

"June has to be in there," Lucas said.

George honked in agreement, his head bobbing up and down.

"We'll go first," Hugo said. "There's no cover here. Nothing to hide behind as we approach. Wait here until we assess the situation. Keep George in the truck. This guy will go after him in a heartbeat. That will severely complicate things."

"Agreed."

Hugo and Milenka approached cautiously. One of them quietly stepped past the doorway so they could flank anyone that stepped outside. Lucas snuck over to the truck Blade had driven there, then back to Thom's truck. George stayed calm inside the truck. He watched the soldiers intently.

Before the soldiers could breach the door, it opened. A voice called from inside. "I'll kill her. Back off!"

They did as instructed. Until they knew what they were up against, it was best to play along. Saving June was the first priority.

Blade stepped out the door. June's hands were bound behind her back and Blade held a knife to her throat. Lucas saw the soldiers look at each other, then to Blade.

We have guns. Looks like you don't. George started squawking loudly.

Thom stayed in the truck trying to calm George down and make sure he didn't try to escape to attempt a rescue of his own.

Blade looked at the bird in the truck, then to June, *I'll kill that one later*.

June kept her demeanor calm and quiet. Inside she was seething, *Not if I have anything to say about it.*

"We're going to get in that truck and you're going to let us leave – or she dies," Blade hissed.

"Can't let you do that." Milenka responded.

Blade was practically dragging June to the truck. She was resisting, trying to distract Blade and throw him off balance.

Lucas watched from the truck, his heart in his throat. "Can't they take a shot?" he whispered.

"Blade's got her too close. She can't pull herself far enough away to give them a shot," Thom replied.

"Can't we just charge him? There's four of us." Lucas already knew the answer. He just didn't like it.

"You know if anyone takes a step toward them, June is dead."

Blade made it to the truck and forced June inside. The soldiers glanced over to Thom and Lucas. Lucas barely nodded his head, but they saw it. They seemed to understand.

Blade put the key in the ignition and turned it. Nothing. Lucas had made sure he wasn't taking that truck anywhere. Blade was furious. He knew getting the truck from Thom wasn't an option. He could never pull that off by himself. He dragged June out of the truck. "We're leaving, and you're not going to stop us!" he yelled.

"Let her go," Hugo said. "You can't win. You'll never make it on foot."

"Oh, I'll win," Blade said. "I made it this far. I'm a survivor. You gonna take a shot and risk hitting her? I don't think so." He started dragging June away from the station.

Thom stepped out of the truck. "Blade, don't do it. Crevasses have developed over the winter. Voids under the snow and ice that you can't see. You won't know you're standing on one until it's too late. It'll swallow you whole."

Blade stomped his foot. "This is frozen solid. We'll be fine."

While being dragged backwards, June spoke to Blade. "You know, your dad got the dagger back. Tosin kept his promise."

"Good," Blade said. "I know I didn't really deserve that from him, after everything I put him through. But it wasn't his to take in the first place, or keep."

Lucas spoke up, "You really think there's anywhere you can go where we won't find you? Think this through Blade. You've been through enough. Give it up."

"I don't think so." He walked backwards, keeping June in front of him. His eyes darting from one person to the other. Hugo and Milenka couldn't get a clear shot. They couldn't risk it. As Blade moved farther away, they joined Lucas and Thom at the truck.

"Any ideas?" one of the soldiers asked.

"We can't let them go far. It's too dangerous. He can't walk backward forever."

Lucas hadn't taken his eyes off of June. He wasn't going to let her out of his sight. Then she disappeared, straight into the ground.

Shit.

Chapter 22:

Crevasse

"Crevasse!" Lucas broke into a run, straight for where he had seen June go down. When he got close, he laid on his stomach to spread his weight out and crawled to the hole. It was the best way to keep more ice from collapsing into the hole.

Thom and the soldiers came up behind him, carrying safety gear that were kept in all of the vehicles. They stayed back, knowing their extra weight could open the void even more. Thom slid Lucas a backpack with ropes, harnesses, picks, anchors and helmets. Lucas knew what to do. It had been part of their safety training.

He tied two ropes to himself and anchored himself into the ice. He threw one rope to Thom. They would try to keep him from falling in.

He crawled to the edge of the hole and peered over the edge. The light on his helmet shined down and illuminated the void. He could see the top of June's head. He could reach her. Thank God. *Please let her be alive.*

"June, can you hear me?"

"Yes." Her response wasn't much more than a whimper.

He turned his head toward the men, "I can see her. She's conscious. I'm going down."

"I'm going to get you out. Just hold on. Can you move your arms? Move very slowly."

"I'm wedged in pretty good. I can't move more than an inch or two. Lucas, I'm pretty sure I'm bleeding."

"Where?"

"My head."

Shit.

He felt the anxiety and uncertainty building inside him. *I can't lose her. I can't go through this. Not again.*

Focus Lucas, he told himself. *You are not going to lose her.*

"June, do you know where Blade is?"

"I can feel something with my boots. I think it's him. He hasn't moved."

George had hopped out of the truck and was squawking and honking and running around like his ass was on fire. Lucas really wished he would shut up. He needed to focus.

"Lucas, I feel really woozy."

"Stay with me June. I need you to stay conscious."

"I'm scared. Lucas, please don't die trying to save me. It's okay to let me go."

"No, it's not okay. Besides, George and Grace would never forgive me."

"You have to protect them." Her voice now had a high-pitched pleading tone.

"We will do that together. They need you. They need to know you're okay. I am not leaving you. I saved Anna and I'm going to save you. I need your help. Can you help me?"

"Yes."

"That's my girl. I'm going to have to crawl down there to get a rope on you. There are three people holding onto me. We'll be fine. We can do this. Stay still. No sudden movements."

"Well, since I can't move that shouldn't be a problem. Is that George? Who's taking care of the egg?"

"Grace. She came back."

"She's going to be such a good mother. Lucas, I'm so tired."

"Stay with me June. I need you. Have you thought of any names for the chick?" He needed to keep her talking and keep her conscious.

"I would like to name it. If that's an option. The staff at the base might want to name it. I don't know." She was speaking more slowly and starting to slur her words. Gotta move fast.

As he lowered his head and shoulders into the hole, snow and ice began falling in. He could hear June's frantic whimpers as it hit her. "It's okay, that's just me crawling in to get you."

"Lucas, I'm right behind you." Thom had made his way to Lucas and was anchoring himself to the ice. Lucas felt much better about crawling into that hole knowing Thom was there to grab him.

He was able to lower himself in far enough to reach June's shoulders. He could see the gash on her head and the blood streaming down her face. She didn't look at him. She kept her eyes closed. Her heart was racing. She was dangerously close to a full-blown panic attack. It was all she could do to hold herself together. She was wedged in so tight, the only thing Lucas could do was feed one end of the rope under her armpit, snake it across her chest and under the other armpit. It was a long process. It was nearly impossible to move in the tight space and he had almost no dexterity with his gloves on. The gloves were slowing him down. He tore them off in frustration. It allowed him to work faster, but he knew it wouldn't take long for frostbite to set in.

He moved slowly and cautiously, knowing June could slip further down at any moment and he might not be able to reach her. The friction from his movements and their body heat made the void more unstable.

At one point June started to slide. She shrieked and Lucas grabbed onto her, supporting part of her weight while he finished securing the rope. Snow and ice kept falling into the hole, making it hard to see what he was doing. Still, he managed. He talked to her the whole time, making sure she responded to keep her conscious. "So, you heard from Suha?"

No response. He yanked on her coat. "Talk to me June. You need to stay awake. Once we're out of here, you can sleep all you want."

June sighed. "Yes. I got an email from her. It was short and cryptic. It said something like 'Mission accomplished. We're with M & D. Everyone is fine. Watch your email for new senders."

"That's good, that they're okay. 'Mission accomplished' means that Tosin returned the dagger. M&D probably means mom and dad. Saif is probably setting up a secure system for them. One that can't be easily traced."

"I thought the same thing."

Once he was sure June was secure, he called up to Thom. "She's secure. Pull us up!"

"Hold on. Here we go."

Lucas grabbed two handfuls of the rope along with June's coat. It was the best he could do until they got high enough that he could try to get a better hold of her. He felt his body moving backward toward the surface. "Please don't let go," June begged.

"I got you," he said. "I won't let go." *Maybe not ever.*

Once the hole was wide enough, he repositioned his grip and soon they flopped onto the ice like a couple of whoppers just snagged by some fisherman. Hugo and Milenka quickly dragged them away from the hole, where they knew the ice could support their weight. The three of them just laid there, staring at the sky. The sun was out, which was a rare sight during the Antarctic winter. For just a moment, Lucas was a child again, floating in the ocean near his home, trying to reach the shore. He pulled his nearly frozen hands into the sleeves of his coat.

"Thank you," June whimpered.

George waddled up and hovered over her, looking down. Honking and dancing happily. "Hi George."

"I'm going to crawl back there to see if I can see Blade," Thom said.

At the edge of the crevasse, Thom shined his light into the void. He could see Blade's head, cocked at an odd angle.

Back at the group he said "His neck's broken. He's too far down for any of us to reach him."

In the truck, on the way back to base Lucas said "Something else has happened, but I'm not sure if I should tell you yet. It can wait."

"Something besides Blade being alive, kidnapping me and Grace coming back?'

"Yes."

"Go ahead. Tell me."

"Sasha is alive. She's at the base. She's being held for questioning. We think she came here with Blade."

Lucas watched the emotions on her face as she processed that information. Sasha is alive? That's wonderful. Wait, she was hiding with Blade? Why? What's going on?

"We don't know anything yet. Cruz may know more. We left to find you as soon as we realized someone else was here."

June nodded and put her head on his shoulder. George cuddled up against her.

"I'm sorry I went by myself. That was really stupid."

"Yeah, it was," Thom replied from behind the steering wheel.

They dropped George off on the way back to base. He marched into the colony, squawking and honking proudly as if recounting the tale to Grace and his neighbors.

"It would have taken us a lot longer to find you if we didn't have George with us. He knew right where to go."

Back at base, the five of them had to report to the medical center for a mandatory evaluation. Lucas's hands had been saved from frostbite. June had to stay for observation and to rule out any other serious injury. Lucas stayed with her. Once June was released, they went straight to their quarters. Everything else could wait until tomorrow. They were both sore and exhausted. Lucas just wanted some peace and quiet and to hold June in his arms.

Once in bed June cuddled up to him as close as she could get. She was like a scared child.

Lucas wrapped his arms around her tightly. He wanted her to feel safe. She went right to sleep.

A nightmare of June's death in the crevasse woke Lucas up with a jolt in the early morning hours. The crevasse was a fiery pit. In the dream, George, Grace and their egg fell into the crevasse as well. Leaving Lucas alone with nothing to live for. He was considering jumping into the pit when he woke up. It felt so real. He was relieved to see June lying beside him. It was only a dream.

June stirred, rolled over and went back to sleep. Now wide awake, Lucas got up, went to the living room and booted up his laptop. He re-visited Sasha's social media accounts. He wanted to understand her life better before they talked to her today.

After an hour of what felt like online stalking, he turned his attention to endangered species. It was a heartbreaking endeavor but an excellent learning experience. According to the internet, there are over 16,000 animal species on this planet that are endangered. Animals that he didn't even know existed, in danger of disappearing from our planet forever. He read several articles on rhinos. The data confirmed what Tosin had said on the ship. Rhinos were in serious trouble. Some species were already extinct or considered functionally extinct. There are so few left in existence it is believed that some species will not survive. He knew that elephant tusks were made of ivory. He learned that elephants are a big target for poachers. For their tusks. And for what? He couldn't find one piece of information confirming that ivory has ever saved a life. Apparently, elephants are still slaughtered so people can display their pretty baubles. There's that word again, greed.

Lucas thought about the sci-fi movies he's seen where aliens invade Earth and start killing humans – and the humans don't like it. If people don't think it's right for another species to kill them, why do they think it's okay for them to kill another species? He couldn't help but wonder; if humans had the ability to travel to other planets and annihilate another species, would they?

He heard a voice, a whisper. It didn't come from another person. Was it coming from him or from somewhere else? He didn't know. Wherever it came from, the message was clear and simple. *Save them.* He stared at the monitor and knew he had to do something.

"Lucas?" He could hear the fear in June's voice.

"I'm here," he said quickly. "Everything's fine. Good morning."

She came into the living room and sat next to him, still groggy. "What are you doing?"

"I woke up early. I went over Sasha's social media accounts; then I moved on to endangered species. You probably already know this, but there are at least 1200 bird species listed as endangered."

"I know. It breaks my heart. What do we do?"

"We fight for them. Turns out we're pretty good at that."

June gave him a loving smile. "Yes, we are." She rested her head on his shoulder, and they just stared at the monitor together.

Chapter 23:

An Unexpected Ally

Cruz contacted them and told them to come to the joda. They got ready and stepped outside. There sat their truck. Back from the vacant station where they had left it the day before. They walked to the joda. The weather was calm enough to walk. Plus, they both loved walking around the base with penguins for company.

"I had forgotten about Sasha until you mentioned it earlier. I have this feeling of dread. Like I already know I don't want to hear what she has to say."

"Me too."

Cruz met them outside. "Good morning. Sasha's inside. She hasn't been questioned yet. Yesterday we let her take a hot shower and eat as much as she wanted. We just let her be. To give her time to think. We don't know what she's done wrong, other than hide out in vacant buildings. We kept her confined, of course. She really doesn't seem like the criminal type to me."

"I was going over her social media accounts this morning," Lucas said. "She was in Tripoli about a year ago. During the off season, when the cruise ships don't come here." Cruz nodded. "Let's hear what she has to say."

"Does she know about Blade?"

"Yes. She asked about him. I told her the truth."

"How did she take it?"

"She seemed relieved."

Inside, Sasha was sitting at a table. Hugo and Milenka were there, acting as guards. When Lucas and June walked in, Sasha looked at the floor. She had the look of a dog that had just been scolded for misbehaving. June's heart went out to her and the feeling of dread disappeared. Sasha looked like a victim, not a criminal. As soon as they sat down, Sasha said, "I am so sorry. I never wanted any of this to happen. I feel like such an idiot."

"Are you ready to tell us what happened?" Lucas asked. Sasha nodded. "Start from when you arrived in Tripoli last year." Sasha looked surprised that Lucas knew she had been in Tripoli. She didn't ask how he knew.

"That's when it started. When I was in Tripoli. I like to travel. To various places and countries to study the different foods that people eat and how they prepare them. Sometimes it's a cooking school; sometimes it's lessons at a restaurant. There's always a group of students. In Tripoli it was lessons at a restaurant. At the end of the day, I went out with a few people from the group. That's when I saw Blade. He was with his friends. I didn't know at the time that was his gang. I thought he was cute. You know, the bad boy type. He saw me looking at him and took advantage of it. It was the first of many times that he would take advantage of me. Anyway, he came up to me, being all sweet and bad boy cool. I was enamored. I was naive. I thought he would fall in love with me and change his ways and we would live happily ever after. That's the downside of watching too many movies and forgetting that movies aren't real. If movies were based on real life, nobody would watch them. He seemed really interested when I told him what I did for a living. I didn't think too much of it at the time. I figured he would just try to score a free trip to Antarctica. Which he did, but not from me. We stayed in touch after I left Tripoli. We talked and texted. He told me how much he missed me practically every day. By the time he told me he was coming on the cruise and we both arrived in Ushuaia, I was completely smitten and would've done anything for him. I realize now that was his plan for me all along. I had a purpose. He needed me complacent. He never told me his plan. He did tell me about his father's dagger; but only that someone else had it and he needed to get it back. We spent the night together in Ushuaia, but once the ship left port, I knew something was wrong. He went into hiding. The only time I saw him was when he needed something. Like he wanted me to bring him food or move something from one place to another without anybody knowing. He was nice to me but the lovely-dovey charade was over. When they found Lucia, I figured he was in on it. I was scared and I wanted no part of it. I went looking for him. I wanted to know what was going on. I was going to pretend I didn't know about Lucia. I found him below, tied up with a bullet hole in his leg. He played the role of a victim perfectly. He could've won an award for that performance. He managed to drag me right back into his web of lies. I untied him and bandaged his leg. By now the crew had a pretty good idea that there was a gang on board preparing to take over the ship. I acted as clueless as I could, playing the role of a scared female. He assured me that he was not part of the gang and wanted no part in taking over the ship. He found out that his father's dagger was on board, and he was there to get it back. That's all. I prepared the food to make the gang members sick, except him of course. The helicopters showed up in the morning and things got pretty crazy. I went to check on him. I couldn't find him. I looked everywhere. I was on deck. I saw you struggling with him. I didn't see everything, but I knew he had done something wrong. I saw him go overboard. Once you guys walked away, I was able to get him back on board before the helicopters spotted him. I should've let him drown. Everyone was at the bow, so I was able to hide him easily. Then we had the party, and the passengers evacuated. The ship didn't head back to Ushuaia immediately. The captain was taking care of some things. I figured it was some extra tasks that came along with almost getting your ship taken over by what I like to call "pirates". It sounds better than a Libyan gang. When I went to check on Blade, he said we had to get off the ship. I thought he was crazy. I told him I wasn't getting off the ship. I was going back to Ushuaia with the crew. He said "No, you're not going to Ushuaia. You come with me, or I'll kill you and throw your body overboard. Either way, you're staying here." She looked at the group. "Tough choice, huh? I gathered as many supplies as I could. We managed to get a lifeboat into the water and off we went. I think we were maybe a quarter mile from the ship when it exploded. I was in shock. I couldn't believe what I was seeing. My heart ached." Her stony exterior cracked. Her voice went up an octave and tears streamed down her face. "Those were my friends. They were my family. I spent more time with them than my real family. I would've never hurt them. I think Blade did it. I thought that all of the weapons had been taken off of the ship. I never asked him. I didn't want to know. At that point I knew I was in hell. We made it to land. Half frozen and half dead. I barely remember finding a vacant building and Blade breaking into it. We brought the supplies in, even though it wasn't much warmer inside than it was outside. No heat. No running water. We found some dry clothes and blankets. That started our quest to survive. Blade was awful. My presence became an annoyance. I'm pretty sure he only kept me alive because he thought he might need me at some point. He constantly complained about another mouth to feed. About me using up his precious supplies. Over time it got worse. We had to move from building to building looking for food and supplies. It got to where I was afraid to go to sleep. I was afraid he would kill me so he didn't have to share what little food we had. One night when he was asleep, I snuck out. I made it to another station without getting caught. I was glad it was so close to your base. I should've just walked up and told my story right then and there. I didn't know what to do. I didn't care about getting caught. I just wanted it to be over. If I had thought for one second that Blade might hurt somebody, I would've turned myself in right away. It didn't even occur to me. I should've known. I wasn't thinking clearly. I'm so sorry."

"Torment and starvation will do that to you. Survival mindset kicks in," Cruz said.

"Sasha, do you think anybody survived the explosion?"

"I doubt it. The ship went down quickly. I didn't see any helicopters around. They didn't show up until after the ship had completely sunk. I didn't watch the ship go down. I couldn't have that vision in my head, haunting me for the rest of my life. There were some zodiacs around when we were trying to get off the ship, but that was before it exploded."

"Thank you for telling us your story. I know it's hard to relive it."

"You all have been so nice to me. I feel like I don't deserve it. I was a zombie walking around in a skeleton's body. I was sure I'd be dead by now. It's good to feel like a human again. Thank you"

"We still have to keep you confined and guarded."

"I understand. I'm fine with that. Compared to what I've been through recently, these are 5-star accommodations."

More questions were asked. Sasha did her best to answer them. Food was served. The small group began chatting about other topics. June took the opportunity to learn more about Sasha and her life before she arrived in Tripoli.

Chapter 24:

It's A Girl!

Winter transitioned to spring. Sasha became a member of the community, with restrictions. Hugo and Milenka became her permanent bodyguards. They were with her almost every waking moment. No one really thought she would ever do anything to hurt anybody, but it was necessary. The orders came straight from the Argentinian government. She must be monitored or confined at all times. Saturday nights at the joda became much more enjoyable. Sasha happily put her cooking skills to good use and meals at the base suddenly got a lot more delicious. Many of the residents commented on how happy they were to have her there. They hadn't eaten this well in months. The topic of conversation on social nights always included the much-anticipated Emperor hatchlings. Residents always asked Thom and June if the eggs had started to hatch, particularly George and Grace's.

"We do have a few new babies at the colony, but George and Grace's little bundle hasn't made an appearance yet."

"Do you think I could be able to go see the colony?" Sasha asked sheepishly. June looked at Hugo and Milenka for their opinion.

"I'm okay with it if you're okay with it," Milenka said. "Gives me an excuse to go too. I'm anxious to see the little fluffballs." Hugo nodded wholeheartedly in agreement.

"It's a date," June said.

"I'm going too," Lucas called out from a few feet away. He had been chatting with Cruz. "I'm starting to feel left out. I want to see the little guy too."

"Or girl," June smiled. "I can't wait to meet their baby."

The next day they ventured out in two trucks. The base strives to not interfere with the penguin's natural way of life, but these were no ordinary birds. Everyone knew the arrival of George and Grace's chick was going to be a very special event, and they didn't want to miss it. All of the residents wanted the chance to see the babies. They couldn't all come at once. They would have to take turns.

They stood at the edge of the colony. They could see the heads of a few chicks poking out from beneath their parents' fur. There were many comments. "There's one." "Look there." "They're so cute!" June's gaze was locked on George and Grace. They were standing together at their nest. She couldn't see an egg or a chick. "I guess theirs hasn't hatched yet." she said with a hint of disappointment. Then George looked down at his feet and gave a soft honk. From beneath his fur, a fluffy little head emerged.

"There it is. It's here!"

George started to toddle over to the edge of the colony with the baby riding on his feet. Not to be left home alone, Grace came too. June slowly sat down. They were bringing their baby to meet her. She was honored beyond words. She had been praying she could experience this since she realized Grace was pregnant on the ship. She couldn't stop the flow of tears that quickly streamed down her face. She didn't want to. She didn't care if they froze on her cheeks. She loved these birds so much. They were like family to her.

"Hello you two. Your baby is beautiful." Her free-flowing tears were dripping from her chin.

The group stayed back and remained quiet. This was June's moment. She had a very special bond with those birds, and no one was going to take that from her. "Have you thought of any names?" Thom asked quietly.

"I was wondering if I would be allowed to name it. I never asked. I know naming them is not encouraged."

"These are very special birds," Cruz said. "The video from the ship went viral. You allowed us to post the 'Say good night Gracie' videos. Those went viral too. George and Grace have become a worldwide sensation. People have fallen in love with them. Their baby needs a name. The world will demand it."

"I need to know if it's a boy or a girl."

"I think I know where you're going with this." Lucas said. She lowered her hands to the ground in front of the chick. "May I?" she asked George. She would not handle the chick without his permission. George lowered his head and gave a soft honk. The chick looked at June's hands, uncertain. George honked again. The chick inched forward, and June gently picked it up.

"It's a girl. Her name is Sandra."

The group looked at Lucas for an explanation. He motioned to the birds. "Our George and Grace are named after George Burns and Gracie Allen. The human George and Grace had two kids, Sandra and Ronnie. I had to look that up."

"So, if our George and Grace have another chick and it's a boy, his name will be Ronnie."

"Exactly." June said. The group began to step forward and peer over June's shoulders, trying to get a better look. Sandra peered up at them and gave a soft squeak. Grace honked in response.

"I think mom is telling her that we're okay."

"I think you're right."

Everyone slowly sat down and simply enjoyed the moment. Thom took photos and videos to commemorate the occasion. June returned Sandra to George's feet. After a few minutes, the new family returned to their nest. Everyone rose and headed to the trucks.

"That is one of the coolest things I've ever experienced. Thank you for letting me be a part of it," Sasha said.

"Yeah, that was amazing." Hugo added.

Everyone was elated and in awe of what had just happened. The mood among the group was electric. "I'd be happy to cook if anyone wants to eat at the joda," Sasha volunteered. "I feel like I couldn't possibly sit still right now."

"Sounds good to me," Thom said. "I'm pretty hyped up, and hungry."

At the joda, the smell of Sasha's cooking filled the air. June helped. She enjoyed cooking with Sasha. She always got some excellent cooking tips. "I've lived alone most of my adult life. I never saw a reason to learn to cook well," June said. "When you live alone, it's easy to fall into the 'grab and go' way of eating. Plus, I grew up in New York City, which is practically the grab and go capital of the world."

"I get that. My mom was a pretty good cook. I think I caught the cooking bug from her. I've never been to New York City. Sounds like a good place for some cooking lessons. I'll put that on my list, if I don't end up in jail."

"I'm not sure you've broken any laws. Made some bad decisions, but they can't throw you in jail for that."

Sasha shrugged her shoulders. "I wonder if Cruz would let me stay here."

"To keep eating your amazing cooking? He would probably consider it, but I don't think it's up to him."

"He let you stay."

"I will be eternally grateful for that, but that was a unique situation. Besides, I'm not sure he's staying. The residents here don't stay long term. Most of the people here will return to the mainland and a new group will arrive for the summer."

"Well, the oil under the Weddell Sea isn't going away, and neither is the desire to drill for it."

"Agreed. I don't think things can just be 'business as usual'. The red flag has been raised. I hope people are paying attention to more than just the cute videos."

"We need to help them see the whole picture." It was Lucas. He had come to check on them.

Sasha looked at them both. Her face lit up. "I'll help. If you guys do a fundraiser, I'll cater it."

"If you're cooking, we could charge top dollar for tickets," June said.

"I'd pay it." It was Cruz, standing behind Lucas. "Your food is so good." Sasha blushed. Lucas and June looked at each other, knowing what the other was thinking. Could there be a romance blossoming here?

Cruz didn't let that moment simmer for too long. He spoke up, "People are paying attention. Governments are paying attention. Member countries of the Antarctic Treaty are taking this very seriously."

Lucas spoke up. "Not too long ago the right to mine in Antarctica was approved." June looked at Lucas, *You've got to be kidding me.*

"Yeah, that was a close one. Fortunately, that was stopped. Just barely," Cruz replied.

"That was before 500 billion gallons of oil were discovered. What do you think is going to happen now?" Lucas asked.

"Countries are going to try to figure out how to control it and profit from it," was Cruz's answer.

"We need to help them see the whole picture," Lucas repeated. "Not just the dollar signs."

"Dollar signs are blinders for humans. It's all they see. Personally, you couldn't give me enough money to give up what I experienced this morning at the colony. It was magical. It was grounding. It was priceless. That is something that I will be eternally grateful for," Sasha said. Cruz looked at her with admiration and respect. Lucas and June looked at each other with that knowing smile.

"If George and Grace have become a worldwide sensation, what does that mean for the base?" June asked.

Cruz chuckled, "Apparently every cruise line that comes here has been inundated with people wanting to know if they will get to come here and meet them."

"That kind of foot traffic can't be allowed," June said.

"Agreed. But we should consider the fact that George and Grace are the best spokesmen, or spokesbirds, for what we are currently discussing. This is their home. Humans are just guests here. They were here first. How do we let their voices be heard without exploiting them?"

There was silence as everyone contemplated the question. He had a point. They had to find a way.

Sasha broke the silence. "Looks like we've got our work cut out for us. Right now, there's hungry people wanting to eat, including me."

Chapter 25:

Farewell

Weeks went by. The weather calmed. The temperature rose. The sun rose for more than four hours a day. Everyone was relieved to come out of the dark, cold winter. The topic of conversation at the joda turned to what the upcoming summer months would bring.

"Ships will be arriving soon with supplies and new residents," Cruz said.

"Is anyone at this base going to stay on over the summer?" Lucas asked.

"Yes. Thom is going to stay. The government has already let us know that more tourists will be allowed here during the summer. People are frantic to see where George and Grace live. We have been pushing to keep those numbers as low as possible. Thom needs to be here to make sure the birds aren't exploited." Cruz looked directly at June. "This is a slippery slope. There's a fine line between letting George and Grace help without exploiting them. Hugo and Milenka are staying too. We need people here who can relay to the new residents what we've been through. It's important that they understand."

Thom added, "The number of people requesting to come here for the summer has skyrocketed. The videos online make it look like this place is all fun and games. Some of the researchers who will be arriving here may not realize what they are getting themselves into. It's hard work."

June looked at Thom. "I trust you to take care of the birds and put them first. I know it won't be easy. You'll get a lot of pressure from people wanting to profit from them."

"That has already started," Thom said.

"Tell them to sell t-shirts," Lucas said.

"That has already started too."

"Promise to keep in touch," June said. "Leaving them will be one of the hardest things I'll ever do." She paused, "I do plan on coming back. Never seeing them again just isn't an option for me."

"You will always be welcome here."

October arrived. Soon the ships bringing supplies and new residents would arrive. After that, the tourists would come. A farewell gathering at the joda was tradition. Cruz gave Sasha the task of planning and execution. He knew she was the best person for the job; and he couldn't wait to eat the wonderful dishes he knew she would make. That woman could turn the blandest and most boring food into a work of art.

The party was held the day before the first ship was scheduled to arrive. June and Lucas had instructions to be on that ship when it returned to the mainland. The mood at the party was mixed. Some people couldn't wait to get back to the mainland, some people didn't really want to leave. Thom was melancholy. He was happy to stay, but he was going to miss his new friends. "On the bright side," he said, "I get to stay with the penguins."

To no one's surprise, Sasha did a great job at planning and execution. There was not a slice of pizza to be found. "No pizza today. We can do better," she said. The makeshift bar was set up with various wines and liquor available. Sasha was acting as bartender when Lucas and June walked up. June did a happy little hop. "I'll have a glass of that lovely Ice Dancer Chardonnay," she practically announced. Lucas couldn't believe how happy having Sasha hand her that glass made her. June grinned at Lucas. "I might have two," she giggled.

"Go for it."

"How about you Lucas?" Sasha asked.

"Can you make me a virgin mojito?"

"I thought you might ask for that, and yes I can." After handing Lucas his drink and gazed at them both with a sheepish, contemplating look. "I hope we're friends."

"We are," they both answered together.

"You're okay in my book," Lucas added.

"Me too," June said.

"Did you make Tony a virgin mojito at the party on the ship?" Lucas asked.

"I did. He said you recommended it." Her face grew sad. "I miss them so much."

June put her hand on Sasha's arm. "I know you have regrets, but I'm really glad you're here."

"Thanks. That means a lot."

"When are you scheduled to leave?"

"Cruz got permission for me to stay until he leaves, so we can be on the same ship together. Since Hugo and Milenka are staying, he will act as my escort." June made sure she didn't look at Lucas. She knew their look would give away their suspicions. They walked away so Sasha could serve the other guests. As soon as they were a few feet away, June's face broke out into a huge grin.

Lucas chuckled. "You are just loving this, aren't you?"

"I can't help it. I'm happy for them. I hope it works out."

"We don't even know if there is anything to work out."

June gave him a knowing smile. "Yeah, we do."

"Okay, we do."

They mingled for a while, saying their good-byes to people they might not see again before they left the next day. Eventually they made their way to Cruz.

"When are you scheduled to leave?" Lucas asked.

"I'm staying until my replacement arrives, and I get him or her up to speed on everything I think they need to know."

"Sasha told us that you'll be returning to Argentina together," June said.

"Yeah. She's going to have to answer for her actions, but I still don't think she'll go to jail." Cruz blushed, "She's from Italy but she's going to stay in Argentina for a while. We've got some things to discuss. See how it goes."

"We wish you both the best of everything. Always," June said.

Later that evening at their quarters, Lucas and June checked their emails. "I got an email from Suha," June said. "She says everything is fine and Saif set them up with a secure email server. She says you should have a very important email that you need to read."

Lucas furrowed his brows, questioning. He opened his inbox and scanned his emails. His heart skipped a beat. There was one email from sender "Penguins Unite". So many thoughts ran through his mind in a split second. Most of the crew knew that phrase. It could be any crew member, but it would have to be a crew member. Someone survived. He couldn't allow himself to hope. It's probably Jakob. He knew that phrase. Still, his gut instinct told him that opening that email was going to change everything. It read:

Hey Lucas,

Surprise! I'm alive. I ended up on the same rescue ship as the Sulimans.

I'll tell you the story when I see you in Ushuaia. I'm going to be there when you and June arrive.

Saif added me to his secure email server. We can be all 'Top Secret, James Bond' here.

I'll bet you can't wait to get on another ship. Safe travels. See you soon.

We have a lot to talk about.

P.S.: Thanks for recommending Sasha's virgin mojito. It was great.

Tony

Lucas stared at the name. Tony. It had to be him. He survived.

"Lucas?"

Lucas turned his monitor so June could read it. He watched her expression change as she read the words and the name at the bottom. Tears welled up in her eyes. "Tony." she whispered, as if saying the name would somehow jinx it. She looked at Lucas, "If Tony is standing there when we arrive in Ushuaia, I'm going to hug him so tight he won't be able to breathe."

"Please don't kill him. We just got him back. Maybe he knows more about what happened on the ship. He might be able to help us put the pieces together."

Chapter 26:

Together

They stood at the edge of the busy Emperor colony, watching the waddle of penguins well, waddle. The colony was crowded and busy, with parents and chicks going about their daily routine. The chicks were about three months old but still unable to swim. Soon they would have their adult feathers that would enable them to glide through the water seamlessly, like their parents. It was a beautiful day. June had her hood down, enjoying the bright sunshine at the beginning of the Antarctic summer. Her hair glistened, the natural highlights reflecting the sun in various shades of copper and gold.

Lucas thought about the events that brought them here. The last six months played back in his mind. The ship. The crew. The friends they had made, and lost. The joy and uncertainty of new beginnings. The pain of unwanted endings. He was not the same man that boarded the Ice Dancer.

They stood in silence for a few minutes; just staring at nature's majesty. The peace and calm that it brought was intoxicating. The brilliant blue sky and majestic mountains were a sight to behold. Hope Bay was calm and glistening. The sunlight reflected off nearby icebergs, making them sparkle like they were adorned with diamonds. Lucas wanted to remember this feeling forever. After six months, neither of them had even begun to get tired of it.

June turned to him, her eyes stern but calm. They held a soft determination that Lucas had seen many times since the first day he met her. She let her eyes wander, taking in everything. The mountains, the penguins, the water and everything in it. She looked him square in the eye. "Let's save them. Together," she said. He couldn't agree more.

The End

The adventure continues. Excerpt from "Save Us" on the following pages.

Acknowledgements

Thank you to my partner, Coll. Without your love and support, this book may have never been written.

Thank you to my mom, for giving me the idea that started the adventure.

Thank you to my family for always believing in me. With a loving and supporting family, I can do anything.

Thank you to my editor, Benjamin X. Wretlind. For making this book better by finding the flaws and showing me a better way.

Thank you to everyone who reads this book and is inspired to do more and be better. We're all in this together.

About the author

Robyn Roy lives in Michigan with her partner and their mini-goldendoodle, Rebel.

She is an animal lover and a huge Star Wars fan.

Save Them is her debut novel.

It introduces you to characters whose adventures will continue in the sequel, *Save Us*.

There is much work to be done.

Excerpt from "Save Us"

"Lucas, I'm pregnant."

It was bound to happen sooner or later. They had been married for a year.

Two-years earlier a cruise to Antarctica had brought them together and nearly cost them their lives. They ended up stranded at El Polo Sur base for an unplanned six-month layover through the harsh and unforgiving Antarctic winter. They had only known each other for two days. They loved every minute of their unexpected hiatus at the bottom of the world. Except when Blade kidnapped June, they fell into a crevasse and Lucas had to crawl in to save her. Now spring had arrived and it was time to leave the place they had called home and the friends they had made. It was time to return to Ushuaia, the southernmost city in South America. Lucas and June knew what ship they would be departing on and when they had to be on it. Saying goodbye to George and Grace was the hardest thing June had ever done. She had grown very attached to the two Emperor penguins who had been put in her care before she boarded the cruise ship. Now home in Antarctica, she knew they were in good hands. The birds had accepted the staff members at the base and had become quite fond of Thom, the base's penguin expert. Lucas and June had stayed away from the birds for weeks until the day of their departure. They were trying to lessen the attachment they had to each other. Neither Lucas or June was willing to leave without saying goodbye to the amazing penguins that had stolen the heart of the entire world. They knew the arrival of tourists on a daily basis wanting to see the birds could be stressful for them. It took all of June's willpower to put on her best smile and pretend like it was any other day. She couldn't let George, Grace, or their beautiful daughter Sandra know how sad she was. They would know something was wrong. After staying at the penguin colony for as long as they could, June finally said "Say goodnight Gracie."

"Honk!"

"I love you guys so much. Be safe and well until I come back. I will see you again."

Lucas recorded it on his phone so June could keep that memory with her always.

June began to sob as soon as they got into the truck to leave the colony.

Lucas put his arm around her shoulder. "They'll be fine, and we will see them again."

"I know. It doesn't matter how many times I told myself this day was coming, or how hard I tried to prepare for it. I still feel like my heart has been ripped out of my chest." Lucas knew there wasn't anything he could do except be there for her. He was going to miss those birds too. They had been through so much together.

As they neared the ship that would take them to Ushuaia, Lucas realized that June wasn't next to him. He turned to see her standing behind him, looking apprehensive. "I need a moment," she said. "I know we'll be fine; but I just don't want to get on that ship."

He extended his crooked arm to her. "We're doing this together. Besides, Tony is waiting for us in Ushuaia," he smiled.

"Tony." she said, smiling. "I can't wait to see him." She looped her arm through his. "Let's do this."

The two-day trip to Ushuaia went smoothly. They were on a nearly empty research vessel since most of the passengers had disembarked at El Polo Sur. No large dining room. No bar. On this ship you ate in the galley or your very small room. The lackluster accommodations didn't bother them. June spent most of her time marveling at all of the lab equipment and data processing software.

They disembarked in Ushuaia and made their way up the pier.

"Lucas, I feel like everyone is staring at us."

"Me too. Are we painted green or something?"

Just then an excited young woman approached them. "Hi. You're Lucas and June, right?" She was dressed in bright trendy colors.

"Um, yeah," Lucas said slowly. He was afraid of what he was signing them up for. He had no idea how she knew who they were.

"Is this your first day back from Antarctica?"

"Um, yeah." How does she know?

Seeing the perplexed looks on their faces the woman replied, "Oh my gosh. You guys are celebrities. The cruise ship, the Libyan gang. It's been all over the internet for months. George and Grace are awesome and Sandra is so beautiful. She's getting so big! You guys are so lucky."

"Thanks," Lucas said. The last thing he wanted to be was a celebrity.

"Can I get a picture with you guys? My friends will never believe it."

"Leave them alone, dear. They've been gone for six months. Give them their space." Thank goodness the girl's mother stepped in and didn't want a picture too.

June looked at Lucas. "All of the videos that the base posted while we were there."

"And the one of us sliding down the deck of the ship."

"The video of you guys sliding down the deck of the ship is the best. I've watched it a hundred times," the girl added.

"Hey folks. I'm here to pick these two up. They need to be debriefed. Official business."

Tony! It was him. Standing there with that mischievous smile.

Tony guided them to the street and the car waiting for them. He was really here, and he was saving the day again.

As they walked toward the street, June noticed a gift shop with many of its items set outside to entice the tourists. George and Grace and Sandra were on t-shirts, coffee mugs, keychains, everything. Tony saw the surprised look on her face.

"Yeah, they're everywhere. Even online. Type George and Grace into a browser search box and you'll get no less than a dozen websites with penguin items to sell. George and Grace are big money. There have been arguments over who has the right to market them. Since they don't really belong to anybody, no decisions have been made about who can exploit their popularity and who can't."

June looked at Lucas with sadness and fear on her face. "What have we done?" she said softly.

Lucas put his arm around her shoulder. "Don't panic. We don't know if this is really a bad thing. Not yet." June nodded, but was still unsure.

Before they got into the car, June threw her arms around Tony's neck and hugged him so tight he struggled to breathe.

"I am so happy to see you. We thought..." she couldn't finish the sentence.

"Yeah, I was dead," Tony said.

"Okay, my turn," Lucas said, motioning to June to give them some space. The men shared a heartfelt handshake and the acceptable good-natured half hug.

As the three of them got into the car, the driver turned to them from the front seat. "Good day Mr. Kalloe, Ms. Hewitt. It's a pleasure to meet you. Welcome back."

"I got us a hotel, but I decided not to rent a car," Tony explained. "So what do you want to do first?"

"We've been living on a small research vessel for two days. I'd be happy with a good place to eat," June said.

"I'll bet the food at the base wasn't very good either," Tony said.

"Yeah, about that," Lucas replied.

"What?" Tony questioned.

"I'd rather not discuss anything in public," Lucas said.

"Fair enough. I got a standard room at the hotel, but you two have a suite. That way there's a living area where we can sit and talk."

"Good idea. Thanks," Lucas said.

After lunch they checked in at the hotel. Tony gave them some time to unwind and re-acclimate themselves to civilized life. Then he knocked on their door.

"So, where should we start? Should we start with your 'Yeah, about that' comment earlier, how I'm still alive or what I know about the sinking of the Ice Dancer?"

"Ice Dancer first."

"I think I know who did it."